*Rachel felt as if she'd come face-to-face
with the ghost of her dead husband!*

Only it was no ghost. It was a solid, flesh-and-blood
male. A male with the same handsome, square-jawed
face, the same piercing gray eyes, the same whip-
hard, broad-shouldered frame, the same unruly dark
hair and deeply bronzed skin.

The same man, she realized in shock, who'd fooled
her five years ago, to her eternal shame, who'd made
her feel things she'd never felt before or since, who'd
haunted her dreams and tormented her waking hours
for the past five years.

Zac Hammond, her late husband's identical twin
brother. The brother she'd met only one time, on
that fateful night, and saw again every time she
looked at her son.

Dear Reader,

Well, it's that time of year again—and if those beautiful buds of April are any indication, you're in the mood for love! And what better way to sustain that mood than with our latest six Special Edition novels? We open the month with the latest installment of Sherryl Woods's MILLION DOLLAR DESTINIES series, *Priceless*. When a pediatric oncologist who deals with life and death on a daily basis meets a sick child's football hero, she thinks said hero can make the little boy's dreams come true. But little does she know that he can make hers a reality, as well! Don't miss this compelling story....

MERLYN COUNTY MIDWIVES continues with Maureen Child's *Forever...Again*, in which a man who doesn't believe in second chances has a change of mind—not to mention heart—when he meets the beautiful new public relations guru at the midwifery clinic. In *Cattleman's Heart* by Lois Faye Dyer, a businesswoman assigned to help a struggling rancher finds that business is the last thing on her mind when she sees the shirtless cowboy meandering toward her! And Susan Mallery's popular DESERT ROGUES are back! In *The Sheik & the Princess in Waiting*, a woman learns that the man she loved in college has two secrets: 1) he's a prince; and 2) they're married! Next, can a pregnant earthy vegetarian chef find happiness with town's resident playboy, an admitted carnivore... and father of her child? Find out in *The Best of Both Worlds* by Elissa Ambrose. And in Vivienne Wallington's *In Her Husband's Image*, a widow confronted with her late husband's twin brother is forced to decide, as she looks in the eyes of her little boy, if some secrets are worth keeping.

So enjoy the beginnings of spring, and all six of these wonderful books! And don't forget to come back next month for six new compelling reads from Silhouette Special Edition.

Happy reading!

Gail Chasan
Senior Editor

Please address questions and book requests to:
Silhouette Reader Service
U.S.: 3010 Walden Ave., P.O. Box 1325, Buffalo, NY 14269
Canadian: P.O. Box 609, Fort Erie, Ont. L2A 5X3

In Her Husband's Image

VIVIENNE WALLINGTON

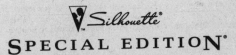

Silhouette®

SPECIAL EDITION®

Published by Silhouette Books

America's Publisher of Contemporary Romance

For John

SILHOUETTE BOOKS

ISBN 0-373-24608-0

IN HER HUSBAND'S IMAGE

This edition published by arrangement with Harlequin Books S.A.

Visit Silhouette at www.eHarlequin.com

Printed in U.S.A.

Books by Vivienne Wallington

Silhouette Special Edition

In Her Husband's Image #1608

Silhouette Romance

Claiming his Bride #1515
Kindergarten Cupids #1596

Previously published under the pseudonym Elizabeth Duke

Harlequin Romance/Mills & Boon

Softly Flits a Shadow #2425
Windarra Stud #2871
Wild Temptation #3068
Island Deception #3095
Fair Trial #3366
Whispering Vines #3656
Outback Legacy #H3817
Bogus Bride #H3911
Shattered Wedding #H4071
Make-Believe Family #H4279
To Catch a Playboy #H4297
Heartless Stranger #H4392
Takeover Engagement #H4585
Taming a Husband #H4663
The Marriage Pact #H4727
Look-Alike Fiancée #H4874
The Husband Dilemma #H4950
The Parent Test #H5111
Outback Affair #H5158

VIVIENNE WALLINGTON

lives in Melbourne, Australia. Previously a librarian and children's writer, she now writes romance full-time. Reading, family and travel are her other main interests. She has written nineteen Harlequin Romance novels under the pseudonym Elizabeth Duke and now writes for Silhouette Books under her real name. Vivienne and her husband, John, have a daughter and son and five wonderful grandchildren. She would love to hear from readers, who can write to her c/o Silhouette Books, 233 Broadway, Suite 1001, New York, NY 10279 or e-mail viv.wallington@bigpond.com.

CAST OF CHARACTERS

Rachel Hammond: Her husband's death had put her in charge of their family cattle station, Yarrah Downs, and she was determined to make it a success. But Zac, her handsome as sin and twice as tempting brother-in-law, kept intruding on her thougths....

Zac Hammond: In the wake of his brother's death this nomadic photographer had finally come home and found Rachel, the one woman who made him yearn to settle down. But the flaxen-haired beauty was a forbidden desire.

Mikey Hammond: An adventuresome little boy sorely in need of a father figure...one he found in his uncle Zac. They shared the same wild streak—and love for Rachel. Little did they know their bond went even deeper than that.

The Saboteur: The nameless, faceless enemy bent on destroying Yarrah Downs. Rachel and Zac would stop at nothing to save the cattle station. If only they knew who it was they were fighting.

Chapter One

"Mummy, will you buy me a gun for my birfday? Then I can go out shooting wild pigs with Vince."

Rachel nearly fell over. "Mikey, you're only three years old—"

"I'll be four in three more sleeps. Vince says I can't go out shooting wif him till I get my own gun."

Rachel silently cursed her head stockman for not telling her son outright that guns and wild-boar hunting were only for grown-ups. Maybe when Vince had children of his own, he'd have more sense. "He meant when you were grown up, Mikey. Only grown-ups can use guns. Come and help me feed the chickens. And let's see how many eggs we can find."

"Okay." Mikey brightened and ran on ahead with Buster, his frisky Blue Heeler.

Rachel vowed to have a word with Vince the minute he returned from checking the water bores. She was already peeved with the sandy-haired stockman for not consulting her more on station matters and making decisions that were rightfully hers. *She* was in charge here at Yarrah Downs now that her husband was gone, not Vince.

But of course Vince didn't expect her to stay on here. Nobody did. Widows with young children weren't usually interested or capable of running outback cattle stations. Especially pampered city-born widows.

Rachel glowered into the dust. The lack of any good spring or summer rains and the continuing hot dry spell was the last straw. If they didn't get some real rain soon, the already low dams would dry up, the parched paddocks would run out of feed and they'd be in even bigger trouble than they already were. A couple of brand-new water bores would help, but she simply couldn't afford them.

As she trudged after Mikey, she heard a light plane coming in. Her father wouldn't fly up here today, surely, three days *before* Mikey's birthday. He would never stay at Yarrah Downs overnight, let alone for *three* nights. He hated the outback, and besides, he was always far too busy running Barrington's.

Her frown deepened. Had he flown up here expressly to try again to talk her into selling and coming back to Sydney? Hedley Barrington never gave up!

She could hear him already. "This is no place for a woman without a husband, or a boy without a father. You can't possibly run this huge, isolated place on your own, Rachel, now that Adrian's gone. Nobody would expect you to.''

She kept telling him that she intended to try, that Yarrah Downs was her home, and Mikey's, too. But she never got through.

''And what about Barrington's? You're my only child, Rachel. Running our chain of department stores is what you trained for and what I've always counted on. I won't live forever—you lost your mother last year and I'm five years older than she was. I want you to come back and help me run Barrington's so you'll be ready to take over when I retire…or shuffle off altogether.''

''Dad, I belong *here*. I love it here. I feel free and at peace. I never felt like that back in Sydney. I felt stifled…suffocated…trapped in a life I didn't want.''

''Rot! You always had everything you could possibly want and all the freedom you could need. I even let you go off and travel the world, on the understanding you'd come back when I needed you. I even let you marry that hick Queensland cattleman of yours against my better judgment. But he's dead now. There's no need for you to stay here any longer. *I'm* the one who needs you now.''

''But I *want* to stay. I'm *going* to stay. Out here in the bush I can *breathe*. I feel alive.''

''How can anyone breathe or feel alive in this heat? In these harsh conditions, without a husband to help you, how can you possibly survive? It won't get any easier, taking on the sole responsibility yourself—it'll get harder, the longer you stay. Don't expect any help from me. I want you back home!''

Rachel kicked up the dust at her feet, shutting her mind to her father's endless arguments. Was she about to hear them all over again?

"I'll just go and see who it is," she called out to Mikey. "You stay with Buster. You can start gathering eggs, but be careful with them!"

The sealed airstrip that Adrian had put in a year or so after Mikey was born and the light plane that had just arrived were out of sight from here. Maybe it wasn't her father. Come to think of it, it hadn't sounded like his Citation jet. Or any kind of jet. One of her neighbors, maybe? Or someone from the bank, heaven forbid! They'd already clamped down on her credit. What next? As if she didn't have enough problems!

She cut across the yard, skirting around the sprawling ranch-style homestead with its shady, vine-covered veranda that still held humiliating memories she hadn't been able to shake, even after all this time.

Her visitor should have had time by now to trudge up from the airstrip. She quickened her steps, weaving through the thick shrubbery and gum trees overhanging the garden path.

A man appeared. She stopped, her eyes drawn to his face. A whooshing sensation swept through her, as if the lifeblood was draining from her.

For a disorienting second, she felt as if she'd come face-to-face with the ghost of her dead husband!

Only, it was no ghost. It was solid, flesh-and-blood male. A male with the same handsome, square-jawed face, the same piercing gray eyes, the same whip-hard, broad-shouldered frame, the same unruly dark hair and deeply bronzed skin.

The same man, she realized in shock, who'd fooled her five years ago, to her eternal shame, who'd made her feel things she'd never felt before or since, who'd haunted her dreams and tormented her waking hours for the past five years, even as she'd tried to despise him, to blot out the shameful memory of him.

Zac Hammond, her late husband's identical twin brother. The brother she'd met only that one time, on that one fateful night, and saw again every time she looked at her son, Mikey.

She began to tremble. "You're a little late." Her voice cracked, but attack seemed the only way to deal with this latest, totally unexpected bolt from the blue. "Your brother's funeral was a month ago."

Adrian's lawyer had notified his absent twin brother of the tragedy, sending Zac word in plenty of time to attend the funeral if he'd wanted to come. When Zac had failed to turn up, she'd assumed he wasn't coming back at all. And she'd been *relieved.* Relieved and irked and bitter and angry, all at the same time.

But mostly she'd been relieved. It was one less problem she would have to deal with. Facing him again, dealing with what his return home would mean...

"I was stuck in a remote part of Zaire, out of contact." His impassive tone gave nothing away. "I headed home as soon as I heard."

But too late...

She drew in her lips. It was so like the excuse he'd

used five years ago when he'd finally made the effort to come home after missing his brother's wedding, not by a day or two, but five *months*. Zac, Adrian had complained on the rare occasions he'd mentioned his estranged, footloose brother, always put his work and his own needs first. He always had and always would.

Zac's priorities, she'd come to realize, were himself first, family last, morals nonexistent. Well, she knew all about Zac Hammond's *morals*. And she'd do well to remember the kind of man he was. She felt her cheeks heating. Had her own morals been so squeaky-clean?

But *she'd* had an excuse. Not knowing Adrian had an identical twin, she'd mistaken the man on her veranda that night for her husband of five months, thinking he'd come home early from his two-week cattle-buying trip down south. The darkness, the hot steamy night and her own foolish romantic yearnings and frustrations had done the rest.

"I wasn't sure I'd find you still here." Zac's sun-sharpened eyes narrowed, raking over her in a way that made her feel he was undressing her, just as he had on that highly charged moonlit night. She took an unsteady step back, another rash of tremors quivering through her. She willed them away, maddened that a mere look could still spark a reaction.

"Oh, you thought I'd have bolted back to the city by now, did you?" *Just like everyone else,* she thought, eyeing him coldly. Not a word of sympathy on the loss of her husband, his own twin brother. Did he think that after the shameful way she'd thrown herself at him the last time he was here, she didn't deserve his sympathy? Did he still believe she'd known all along who he was?

She clenched her hands in suppressed fury, offering him no sympathy, either. He didn't deserve it. He and Adrian might have been identical twins, but they'd never been close, never had time for each other, never had a single thing in common.

"If you thought I'd already gone back to Sydney, why did you come back to Yarrah Downs?" The second the words were out of her mouth, the answer struck her. He wanted to see what he could salvage from his twin brother's estate. From his old family home.

Maybe he even had thoughts of buying the property himself if it came up for sale.

Not to live here permanently, of course. Zac, with his remote work in the wilds, wasn't the settling-down type. But having lived here in the past, he might still have some sentimental attachment to Yarrah Downs and want to keep it in the Hammond family. The vast central Queensland property had belonged to their father, Michael, and to their grandfather before that, before it passed to Adrian.

He could always put a manager in charge in his lengthy absences. Vince would be a prime candidate for manager.

Her breath burned in her throat. The sooner she disillusioned Zac the better! "Well, as you can see, I *am* still here. And I intend to stay. But you're welcome to a bite of lunch before you go. How did you know, by the way, that we had an airstrip here now?"

Five years ago, he'd been driving a rented four-wheel-drive vehicle that had fooled her into thinking it was Adrian's when it pulled up outside the homestead. As *he'd* fooled her when she first set eyes on him in the heady moonlit darkness.

Zac quirked an eyebrow. "I checked when I landed in Brisbane to see how far things had progressed here over the past five years. Nearly five, to be precise."

Rachel's skin broke out in a prickly sweat. Oh, my God, he remembered it was just under five years ago! Four years, nine and a half months, to be exact.

She thought of Mikey and felt a flare of panic. Would Zac guess the truth when he saw her son? *Their* son? But how could he know or guess, even if he saw the amazing likeness? Mikey was the spitting image of the only father he'd ever known—her husband, Adrian, Zac's identical twin brother.

"I didn't know you could fly a plane," she said, quick to change the subject.

"I got my pilot's license four years ago. It's handy to know how to fly when you do a fair bit of flying in small planes."

She shivered, having a sudden vivid image of the life Zac must have been leading over the past years— the dangers, the isolation, the remote areas he must have ventured into to photograph his wild animals. And the lack of human contact, the lack of responsibility to anyone but himself. A reckless, irresponsible adventurer, Adrian had called his brother.

But at least, by burying himself in the wilds, Zac wasn't hurting anyone but himself. He only hurt people when he came back to civilization.

She scowled. She must keep remembering that, remembering how unthinking and unscrupulous he was. Already, just by seeing him again, she was feeling things she didn't want to feel, things she *mustn't* feel.

''So you're still living and working in the perilous wilds? You haven't married and settled down, obviously.'' Regretting the comment the moment it left her lips, she swung her gaze to the sky, pretending an interest in a brilliant scarlet-and-blue parrot overhead. What did she care what Zac was doing with his life? She just wanted him to go.

Not waiting for an answer, she said briskly, ''Well, I guess you'll want to return your charter plane before dark, so we'd better stop prattling and have some lunch.''

''I don't need to return the plane for a couple of days. I was hoping—having found you still here— that you might put me up for a night or two.''

His words stopped her in her tracks. Let him stay here *overnight?* Possibly *two* nights? This was getting worse by the second! To have him sleeping under the same roof! But how could she refuse? He was her late husband's brother after all, and alienated as the two brothers had been, Zac must have felt *something* at the loss of his twin.

She gulped hard and came up with a compromise. ''I guess you could bunk down here, just for tonight.'' It wasn't very gracious, but what did he expect after what had happened the last time he was here?

She almost moaned aloud. She'd tried so hard to forget that shameful night, to pretend it had never happened, but there'd been reminders every day since. Her own heated dreams…her husband's inadequacies…and Mikey. Above all, Mikey.

"Only for one night? After I've come all this way?" Zac's eyes glinted like pewter under her baleful gaze. "You're not going to kick me out the way you did five years ago, are you, before I've even had a chance to look over the place? That wouldn't be very…sisterly."

Sisterly! As if there'd ever been anything the least bit sisterly between them! Just one fevered, uncontrollable night of passion.

She felt heat surge into her cheeks. How dared he remind her of that mortifying night! It just showed he was no gentleman. But she already knew that. Adrian had always said his brother was uncivilized and untamable and did whatever he wanted, caring for nobody but himself. She'd seen firsthand evidence of it.

"You'd better go inside and clean up." She spoke curtly. "You can stay in the guest room next to the bathroom. The room's always made up and ready—for guests who blow in," she added deliberately, her eyes telling him that he could blow out again as soon as he liked. "I need to finish up out here. Be in later." She turned on her heel and headed back the way she'd come, across the yard to the chicken shed.

She would have to prepare Mikey for the shock of meeting an unknown uncle—an uncle who was the spitting image of his dead father. Thank heaven Mikey had stayed out of sight until now. At least she had the chance to warn him.

As Zac strode back to the plane to fetch his bags—mainly photographic equipment, with only a small bag for his few personal belongings—he found himself fighting a gamut of emotions, none of them comforting. He'd hoped to feel nothing at all.

It was a shock to find Rachel still here. He hadn't really expected to, though deep down he'd wanted her to be here. Wanted and dreaded it at the same time, nagged by an unwanted but overriding need to resolve the torment that had plagued him for the past five years.

He'd tried to erase his memory of her, initially by sheer will and ultimately in the arms of other women—on the rare occasions he'd had the opportunity. But it hadn't worked. Rachel had haunted his thoughts and dreams in a way no other woman ever had. And it had been hell, because she was married to his brother and the guilt of what he'd done, losing control the way he had, had left a bitter scar in his heart and mind, a scar that, far from disappearing over the years, had grown only deeper.

Even when he'd heard that his brother had been tragically killed and that Rachel was widowed, he'd hesitated to come back. The inexcusable wrong he'd perpetrated on his brother—that he and a passionate, love-starved Rachel had perpetrated together—still tormented him, and he knew it would always be there between them, whatever happened in the future.

Yet he hadn't been able to stay away. He hadn't been able to forget the powerful feelings she'd stirred in him, the unbridled passion that had spun him completely out of control for the first and only time in his life. Only by seeing her again would he know if those feelings had been real, or simply magnified in his mind over the years.

As they could have been. It wasn't every day a beautiful, half-naked woman threw herself at him—especially in his line of work, where he was more likely to be confronted by a hairy, naked gorilla. He was lucky even to see a woman for weeks and months at a time.

Yeah, that was more likely all it had been—a buildup of sexual need, raging, out-of-control hormones and the sweltering heat of that hot summer's night, as he'd tried to tell a distraught Rachel as soon as reality had hit and they'd both been able to think straight. He'd been trying to convince himself ever since.

He'd had to come back to find out.

His first glimpse of her had blown that convenient theory to bits, proving that the mere sight of her still profoundly affected him, still sent blood racing through him, far hotter and more potent than any feelings of lust he'd had for any other woman.

It was the first time he'd seen her in daylight. Her clear, long-lashed eyes were as blue as a field of cornflowers, her braided hair a gleam of gold under the hot Queensland sun. He'd found it hard to take his eyes off her, harder still to resist those soft lips, lips he'd tasted once and never forgotten.

So he'd better take care. He'd better take mighty good care, or he'd blow everything, just as he'd done the last time.

Rachel had baked bread that morning and made a large pot of soup, using her own homegrown vegetables and herbs. She hoped that the aroma, as Zac ambled into the kitchen while she was preparing lunch, would turn his thoughts to food and away from his first meeting with—she gulped, refusing to think of Mikey as his son—his nephew, who was already at the table, chomping away at a beef sandwich.

Only she knew the embarrassing truth—her own doctor didn't even know—so there was no danger of Zac's finding out unless she showed something in her face, and she'd had years of practice at masking that.

But it wouldn't be so easy with Zac, because he knew her shameful secret, even if he was ignorant of the consequences, whereas Adrian had never known. Her husband had never even suspected, even when they'd failed to have another child. He'd blamed fatigue or overwork after his long days out on the station or even some medical problem of *hers,* never imagining that *he* might be at fault, possibly even infertile, which she'd finally begun to suspect. They'd been married for more than five years and he'd never made her pregnant. Mercifully, *he* hadn't known that.

"Take a seat at the table, Zac," she said, busying herself at the kitchen counter so she wouldn't have to face him yet. "Help yourself to some bread while I slice some more cold meat and pour you some soup. And say hi to your nephew, Mikey. We named him after Adrian's father. Well, your father, too, of course. I've already told Mikey he has an uncle who looks like his daddy, but forgive him if he stares."

Oh, heck, she was babbling. She forced herself to slow down. "This is your uncle Zac, Mikey, your daddy's twin brother," she said as Mikey gaped at Zac. "If you're a good boy, Uncle Zac might tell you about the wild animals he photographs in the jungle," she said to give him something else to think about. Mikey was crazy about animals.

"Have you seen lots of lions and tigers?" Mikey asked in awe, breaking into Zac's friendly greeting, which to Rachel's relief sounded perfectly normal and unsuspecting. She relaxed a trifle.

"Yes, lots."

"Tell me, Uncle Zac. Tell me *now*."

With a slow grin, Zac launched into a string of colorful tales of close, dangerous encounters that held the boy spellbound. Rachel relaxed even more. She even felt able to join them at the table, seating herself at the far end to avoid facing Zac.

"I wish I could go hunting lions," Mikey said as Zac paused to take a few mouthfuls of soup. "I'm going to when I grow up."

Rachel felt a prickle of alarm. Her son had always had an independent, adventurous spirit—a wild streak, Adrian had often worriedly called it. Mikey was a child with boundless energy, forever getting into mischief—so unlike Adrian, who'd always been the quiet, steady, cautious type, a man who thought things through before taking action. Had Mikey inherited his reckless spirit from his father? His *real* father?

"I thought you wanted to muster cattle and break in horses?" she reminded her son.

"I want to do that, too," Mikey said at once. "Can you ride, Uncle Zac?"

"Sure can. I was brought up with horses. Ever ridden a horse yourself?"

Mikey pulled a face. "Not on my own. Daddy wouldn't let me. He said I'm too little. But I'm not. I'm nearly—"

"Mikey, drink your milk." Rachel hoped she'd muffled her son's "four" before Zac could catch it. "Then take this big soup bone out to Buster and check his water. And then you can take him for a run to see Uncle Zac's plane. Well, it's not really his own plane, he's just—"

"Actually, I'm thinking of buying it," Zac put in, cool as you please.

Her heart stopped. "Why would you want to buy a plane? You work on the other side of the world."

"It just happens that my next assignment's here in Australia. The wilds of far-north Queensland and the Northern Territory." There was a teasing glint in his eye, a roguish look she'd never seen in Adrian's more serious gray eyes. "I was hoping you might allow me to use Yarrah Downs as my home base."

"Yeah!" The exultant cry burst from Mikey. "You can teach me how to ride, Uncle Zac. On my own."

Rachel was glad she was sitting down. A wave of light-headedness was washing over her, making the room spin. She could feel a weakening in her bones, as if they were dissolving.

"You're going to work *here?* In *Australia?*" She tried to take it in and what it could mean. So he hadn't come back merely to pay his respects to his brother's widow or to reclaim his old home. He'd come back here to *work*. How stupid to think he might have wanted to see *her*. Work always came first with Zac Hammond, Adrian had often said, in the derisive tone he'd used when speaking of his absent brother.

"Yeah...and it's high time," Zac drawled, his eyes dwelling on her face for a disconcertingly long moment. "There's plenty of unusual wildlife in Australia. Much of it highly venomous." The way his gray eyes glinted made *him* look highly venomous.

Unlocking her tongue, she asked, "For...for how long?"

"As long as it takes. I don't have a deadline. I'm my own boss." Zac let his gaze slide away as he spoke, clearly satisfied that at least he'd given her something to think about.

As long as it takes. Rachel swallowed and pushed her plate away, her appetite gone. Zac's assignment could take months, even years, if his previous assignments were anything to go by.

And in those months or years, he could turn up at Yarrah Downs at any time, staying just long enough to stir her body and emotions and revive memories she didn't want revived before disappearing again, leaving her burning and riddled with renewed guilt for still having feelings for her late husband's twin brother, a man she didn't admire or respect or even like.

"I've finished my milk, Mummy." Mikey put down his empty mug with a clatter. "Can I take the big bone out to Buster now?"

"Here." She pushed back her chair and stepped over to the bench. "Give it to him away from the house," she said as she handed it to him.

"Ta! See you, Uncle Zac!" The kitchen door slammed behind Mikey, rattling the windows.

"Don't bang the door, Mikey!" she called after him, but it was a halfhearted, affectionate protest. Her son never walked when he could run and never closed doors without banging them. That was just Mikey.

"Fine boy you have there, Rachel," Zac commented as she turned back to the table. "The image of his father. And his uncle, come to that."

Her heart missed a beat. With effort she managed to find her voice. "Yes, Adrian was chuffed that his son looked so much like him. He adored Mikey." Adored and despaired of him, convinced that his son's exuberance would lead him to disaster one day.

"Seems to have plenty of energy. How old is he? I can never tell with kids."

This time her heart stopped altogether. "Three," she said, gathering plates and swinging away from the table to avoid looking at him. No need to mention that Mikey would be four in three days. By then Zac would be gone. Back to his solitary life among the wild animals and birds that meant more to him than any home or human being ever had or ever could.

He *would* be gone by then, wouldn't he? *Put me up for a night or two,* he'd said. Not *three* nights.

"When do you start your assignment?" she asked. "Tomorrow? The next day?" After that, hopefully, she'd have some breathing space. She mustn't panic! She'd rarely see him while he was working here in Australia, in the wilds of the far north. He only wanted to use his old home as a base. What his fleeting visits would do to her she refused to think about.

"The starting date will be up to me—or maybe you." Zac reached for another slice of bread. "I'd just like to draw breath here for a few days first, maybe help you out a bit..."

A *few* days now, not just one or two! She felt her stomach knot as she realized that the longer Zac stayed, the more likely he'd be to find out that Mikey was four, not three, as she'd let him think.

But that still needn't mean he'd suspect the humiliating truth. For all Zac knew, her husband could have made her pregnant at around the same time as Zac's brief, ignominious visit.

Zac need never know that Adrian had been rushed to a hospital with acute appendicitis the day after Zac's late-night visit, and that he'd caught an infection and hadn't felt up to having sex for a month after he'd come home—by which time she'd known she was already pregnant. She'd delayed telling Adrian and been deliberately vague about the due date, hoping that her first baby would arrive late, which Mikey conveniently had.

Adrian had never suspected the mortifying truth, and Zac mustn't, either. It was inconceivable to think of Zac Hammond, the irresponsible, unprincipled black sheep of the family, as Mikey's father. Adrian had been the reliable, steady, home-loving brother, the kind of man any woman would have been proud to have as the father of her child. At least—

"Tell me what happened, Rachel." Zac's voice intruded, softly compelling.

"Happened?" Her throat tightened. Did he mean four years and nine and a half months ago, after she'd ordered him to leave Yarrah Downs and never come back? She could still remember Zac's cold, flat words as she'd turned away from him before he could glimpse any other emotion in her eyes than anger— anguish, yearning or even regret. *I'll stay out of your life, Rachel, you can count on that. You and your husband have nothing to fear from me.*

"All I've heard is that he was killed in a tractor accident." Zac spoke gently, jolting her back to reality. He must have assumed, by her choked silence, that she was thinking of her late husband, not, thankfully, of *him.* "How the hell could that have happened? Adrian was the most safety-conscious man I ever knew. He never took risks."

Rachel's heart settled back into place. Of course Zac would want to know about her husband's fatal accident. He was Adrian's twin, after all.

"Not normally, no," she agreed. She'd often wondered if Adrian had had something on his mind that day, some niggling doubt about what he was about to do that had diverted his attention for a fatal second. A second was all it had taken.

"He'd hired a bulldozer—it wasn't a tractor—and had taken it up to Bushy Hill to do some work there. Apparently he was working on the steep lower slope of the hill when the bulldozer hit a huge wombat hole and tipped over. He was thrown out and…and crushed." Cute and furry as the burrowing native wombats were, they did a lot of damage with their holes.

"What was he doing up at Bushy Hill with a bulldozer?" Zac was frowning, she noticed. He looked more angry than pained or sympathetic. "It's supposed to be an animal and bird sanctuary and to be left untouched, in its natural state."

She raised her brows. She'd known there was a lot of native wildlife in the thick scrub and eucalyptus forest of the big sloping hill, but a *sanctuary?* This was the first she'd heard of it. All she knew was that kangaroos and other animals had a habit of jumping or climbing under the fence skirting the cattle paddock below to drink at the small dam there, and that Adrian had been forever mending the fence.

"Adrian wanted to turn the hill into a vineyard," she told Zac. "He said it was ideally positioned to grow vines—facing the right way and that kind of thing. He'd gone up there to start clearing the trees and undergrowth—"

"He intended to turn Bushy Hill into a *vineyard?*" Zac's expression turned thunderous. "Our father made it quite clear to us that the hill was to be left as an animal and bird sanctuary. How much bush had Adrian cleared before his accident? Had he knocked down any trees? Have *you* gone ahead with it?"

She bristled. What right had Zac Hammond to come back after all these years and start bawling her out for something that was no business of his? He'd never even been interested in the family property, according to Adrian.

"No, I haven't." She snatched up Zac's empty plate and whisked it away without asking if he wanted more. "Nobody's touched the hill since. We couldn't afford to, for a start—"

"You're saying you still intend to go ahead with the vineyard when you *can* afford it?"

She glowered at him. "I didn't know it was a sanctuary...or that it was meant to be kept as a sanctuary. Naturally, if that's true—"

"Adrian never *told* you?"

She clamped her lips together. It didn't feel right to be talking about her husband's failings when he was no longer here to defend himself.

Zac swore softly. "I'll need to see how much damage has been done. If he's destroyed that hill and driven the birds and animals out..."

"What do *you* care about Yarrah Downs or what we do with the place?" she flung back. "Adrian said you couldn't get away from here fast enough."

Zac shrugged, drawing her reluctant gaze to the breadth of his shoulders. The same shoulders she'd once kneaded with feverish fingers and dug her fingernails into with frenzied yearning. She flinched and snapped her gaze away.

"Yarrah Downs couldn't have two bosses," he said mildly. "Especially two bosses who disagreed on most things. My father left the property to Adrian because being a cattleman was all he'd ever wanted to be, while I wanted to see and do other things before I thought of settling down in one place. And my brother was good at his job. He had the skill and experience a cattleman needs, even if he lacked judgment in certain areas."

"While you were never interested!"

"Not true. I lived here for most of my life. I spent my childhood here and all my vacations. It was only when my father died and left the property to Adrian that I stopped coming back—except for that one time, a few months after he married you. He'd written to tell me about the happy event. It seemed a good time to finally shake hands and let bygones be bygones.''

His eyes caught hers and she flushed, remembering his short-lived visit five years ago. What had happened between them had put an abrupt halt to any happy brotherly reunion. And she couldn't put all the blame on Zac. She'd virtually seduced him!

To cover her embarrassment she blurted, ''You must have resented the fact that Adrian inherited everything. Is that why you've always been so jealous of your brother and so hostile toward him?''

''Where did you get that idea? From Adrian? I was never jealous of him. We just didn't get on. Too different. Chalk and cheese. I assure you I haven't been seething with resentment all these years. I didn't miss out. My father left me a generous cash pay-out and a bundle of blue-chip stock that's grown over the years. I've also made a lot of money from documentary films and feature articles. I can afford to help you, Rachel.''

Her eyes sparked. ''To help Yarrah Downs, your old home, don't you mean? You don't want to see it go under, and you think it will, now that *I'm* in charge. A woman! What's your secret agenda, Zac Hammond? Are you trying to sweeten me up so you can buy me out if I sell, like everyone expects? Though why you'd want the place...''

Her voice trailed off as she became aware of a dog barking outside. ''It's Buster,'' she said, glad of the diversion. "Mikey must be back. Excuse me… I have things to do out in the yard."

"I'll come out with you. Mind if I borrow a motorbike, Rachel?"

She paused, frowning. "What for?" Did he want to check up on the state of the cattle and the paddocks to see what a mess she was making of the place? So he could criticize her some more, undermine her confidence some more?

"I want to see what damage has been done to Bushy Hill and if there's anything I can do to salvage it."

"Anything *you* can do?" She tried to sound withering—what right had he?—but how could she blame him for wanting to check? This had been his home once and the animal and bird sanctuary clearly meant a lot to him. And if his father *had* specified that it be kept as a reserve…

Funny that Adrian had never mentioned it. Had he thought she might try to stop him from planting his vineyard there? She probably *would* have tried if she'd known about the sanctuary. The thought of her husband keeping things from her was sobering. *But hadn't she kept far worse secrets from him?*

She hadn't been back to Bushy Hill since Adrian's fatal accident. She wasn't sure how much clearing her husband had done. She'd simply told Vince to stay away from the hill until she decided what to do with it. They had more-urgent priorities. But the truth was, to have squashed the idea of the vineyard outright would have felt like crushing Adrian's dream.

Only now that she knew the facts…

"Quiet, Buster!" she shouted over the dog's barking, wondering why he was making such a din. What was Mikey doing to him?

But when she stepped outside, Mikey was nowhere in sight. The yard was empty. "Where's Mikey?" she cried as Buster's barking grew even more frenzied at the sight of her. He started to run off, then wheeled back, whining and pawing at her, before scampering off again.

She got the message and broke into a run. "Something's happened to Mikey!" The words whipped over her shoulder at Zac. "Find him, Buster!" she urged the cattle dog. "Take me to Mikey!"

Chapter Two

As she rushed across the yard in Buster's wake, she heard faint screams—a child's petrified screams.

"Mikey!" she cried out. Where *was* he?

She faltered, her blood running cold. Ahead, down past the sheds, stood the big windmill, its glinting blades whirling in the warm May breeze. A small dark shape was huddled way up near the top, crouched on the uppermost rung of the narrow steel ladder, dangerously close to the rotating blades.

Oh, dear God. Mikey!

She felt Zac's hand on her arm, steadying her, his touch, even in her panicked state, bringing a tingling heat to her skin.

"Try to be calm," he rasped in her ear. "Don't let

him see how scared you are. You don't want him to panic.''

Biting down on her lip, she covered the remaining ground at a sprint, managing not to scream at the terrified boy. Buster reached the windmill first, his barking giving way to whimpers and whines as he circled the foot of the steel ladder.

''Mummy's here, Mikey. Don't move!'' Rachel called. Perilously close to him, the whirling blades glinted ominously in the midday sun, sending a black, twisting fear through her. ''I'm coming up to get you.'' She spoke reassuringly, though she had no idea how she would be able to hold on to her son and keep a firm grasp on the narrow steel ladder at the same time. ''Don't look down!''

She felt Zac's hand on her shoulder, easing her to one side. ''I'll climb up and get him, Rachel. I'm stronger. I'll keep him safe, I promise.''

Would he? She gripped his arm in agonized indecision. Would he be as careful as she would be, the boy's own mother? Mikey meant everything to her, but what did he mean to Zac? He'd never met the boy until today, and he only knew Mikey as the son of a brother he'd never had any time for, a nephew he'd known nothing about until today.

But Zac *was* strong, far stronger than she was. With those powerful hands and shoulders he'd be more likely to bring Mikey down safely. She must trust him. She must trust the man who'd shown he wasn't worthy of trust by betraying his own brother, as she'd unknowingly betrayed her own husband. But this was a matter of life and death, not morals.

"Please…take care," she whispered, and let her hand drop away.

"I will, don't worry." He started scaling the ladder, his strong, tanned hands gripping the rungs in a way that gave her a measure of comfort. She'd felt those same hands on her body and knew they could be gentle, too….

She held her breath, clenching her teeth in a frenzy of suspense. Zac was nearly at the top now and she could hear him speaking gently to Mikey. Her heart leaped into her mouth as he managed to loosen Mikey's frightened grip on the ladder and gather him in one arm, keeping his other hand firmly on the ladder. And then they were coming down, Mikey's arms curled around his rescuer's neck and his small plump legs wound around Zac's upper body.

Rachel didn't start breathing again until they were nearly at ground level, close enough for her to catch her son if he fell. She let her gaze dwell for a second on Zac's strong, competent arms and broad shoulders, feeling a rush of gratitude.

The wayward thought popped into her head that Adrian, if he'd been here, instead of Zac, would probably still have been hesitating down below, or calling for backup, or putting a detailed plan into action, weighing up the pros and cons before acting—always the safe, precautionary approach, so different from his more risk-taking, man-of-action brother.

And who was to say which approach was the best? On the one hand, Zac could have lost his grip on Mikey or the ladder as he'd come down, while on the other, her son could just as easily have panicked and fallen while Adrian was preparing a rescue plan, with safety harnesses and bales of hay to provide a soft landing if the worst happened.

But all that mattered was that Zac had brought her son down safe and sound, without any delay or fuss at all. When the two reached solid ground, she gathered Mikey in her arms and held him tightly for a long moment, her eyes moist as they sought and found Zac's.

"Thank you," she said, and felt a tiny frisson of shock as his eyes caught and held hers for a heart-stopping second before she broke eye contact.

She could feel Mikey's weight dragging on her arms and shoulders and was thankful she hadn't been forced to bring him down from that great height herself. Already he was wriggling to be put down, which only added to his weight. She set him on the dusty ground but didn't release him, instead placing her hands on his shoulders and leaning over to bring her face close to his.

"Mikey, you know you're not to climb up the windmill. I've told you a hundred times. We've all told you. It's far too dangerous. Why did you do it?"

His answer floored her. "I was spotting tigers from the treetops, like Uncle Zac."

Like Uncle Zac... She tossed her brother-in-law a sharp glare, her gratitude disintegrating. Damn Zac and his exciting tales of wild animals. Already he was causing trouble and exerting a dangerous influence on her son.

"Mikey, there are no tigers in Australia. And a windmill is not a treetop."

"Just a boy's lively imagination." Zac's tone was benign, not the least concerned or penitent. "I was just the same. Always dreaming of adventure and excitement and travel to exotic places. Always getting up to mischief. Mikey must have inherited his high spirits from his uncle." He said it with a certain amount of satisfaction.

Rachel's heart did a double flip. "He's more likely to have inherited it from me," she said in her most squashing tone. "I was a tomboy as a kid, always getting up to pranks. But putting yourself in danger is a different thing entirely. I'm trying to raise my son to be responsible."

"You can be too cautious, too careful, Rachel. It can make you vulnerable, tighten you up, cause you to make mistakes. Look where caution got Adrian."

She sucked in a vexed breath. "That was a freak accident. It could have happened to anyone. It had nothing to do with being too cautious and tightening up."

"Maybe. Or maybe he felt guilty about what he was doing to Bushy Hill and lost concentration just long enough to make a lethal mistake."

She snapped her mouth shut. Hadn't she had a similar thought herself?

Adrian had always tended to put the needs of the cattle station ahead of conservation and the rights of native animals—"vermin," he'd called them. He'd been forever complaining about the kangaroos, wallabies and wombats and the damage they caused, kicking down fences and digging holes that tripped the horses.

And her husband had had a point. The wildlife often did cause problems. Only yesterday Vince and her young jackeroo, Danny, her recently arrived apprentice farmhand, had found a dead kangaroo in one of the outlying dams. If they hadn't discovered it so quickly, by a sheer fluke, it could have polluted the water over time. Especially with the dam so low.

Worse, the dead kangaroo had been shot. Its body must have been deliberately thrown into the dam. She couldn't imagine anyone at Yarrah Downs doing such a thing and had put the incident down to intruders, trespassing onto the property at night to hunt wild boar and shooting the 'roo in frustration after failing to find what they were looking for.

Her chest swelled in a sigh. Since her husband's death, nothing had gone right. It had been one problem after another.

"You can take Adrian's motorbike," she told Zac. "It's in that shed over there." She waved a hand. "You'll find bottles of water in the cool room in the same shed. Better take some with you." She paused. "Let me know what damage has been done and I'll see what we can do about it."

"Whatever damage has been done," Zac said grimly, "I'll fix it—if it's not too late."

"Can I go with Uncle Zac?" Mikey begged. "Dad used to let me ride on his motorbike."

Only once, Rachel recalled, and only around the homestead yards. Her husband had decided it wasn't safe. Safety had been paramount to Adrian. Until he'd made his one fatal mistake.

"No, you can *not* go, Mikey." Best to keep him

under her eye and away from Zac. Away from further trouble. "You can stay here and help me. And later I might give you a ride on Silver."

Adrian had bought the pale-gray gelding for her as a wedding gift, after she'd told him she'd taken riding lessons for years and had competed in show-jumping events. On the rare occasions she could find someone to look after Mikey for a few hours, she loved taking Silver out on musters or for invigorating gallops to blow the cobwebs away and feel the wind in her hair. More and more often lately, at Mikey's urging, she'd been letting her son ride around the yard on Silver.

"Wifout a lead?" Mikey gave her a beseeching look.

She hesitated. Silver was a big horse and could be hard to hold. But if they stayed in the yard and she stayed close by…

"If you do as I say."

Zac gave a quick grin, as if he'd helped Mikey win a point. "Well, be seeing you."

As he ruffled the boy's dark curls and strode off to the shed, Rachel let out another sigh, remembering Zac's comment about her husband's assault on Bushy Hill. *If it's not too late,* he'd said, in a harsh tone. There'd plainly been little love lost between the twin brothers.

Zac raised a trail of dust as he roared across the paddocks. His brow was lowered, but he wasn't thinking of Adrian. He was thinking of Rachel. She clearly didn't want him here. She hadn't forgiven him. He'd be lucky if she ever did. And how could he blame her? Hadn't he been blaming himself for what had happened on that highly charged night ever since?

He let out a savage groan. The only woman he'd ever wanted, ever cared about, ever lost his head over, and she could never be his, even now that she was free. She would never be able to forgive him or trust him again. She despised him. Damn his stupidity, his weakness, his pathetic loss of control. Damn it to hell!

Even now, he couldn't understand how it had happened. Nothing like that had ever happened to him before. No woman had ever had that kind of power over him, making him forget everything but his scorching need for her and the mind-numbing, earth-shattering way she affected him. He'd always prided himself on his strength of character, his integrity, his loyalty.

But they'd deserted him the moment his brother's wife had thrown herself at him and pressed her fevered lips to his, at the same time running her hand down his body and over his shorts, boldly gripping him, setting off a reaction he would never have believed possible. Some power or demon stronger than himself had taken possession of him.

If only he'd stayed away five years ago, today could have been their first meeting...and she just might have looked on him differently, despite what she'd heard about him from Adrian. At least she could have made up her own mind, with no preconceived ideas of her own to influence her.

But now it was too late!

He put his foot down even harder, almost flying through the air as he deliberately increased his speed, heedless of the danger, not caring in that black, reckless moment what happened to him. Even if he broke his neck, who would care?

And then he thought of Mikey, his nephew, a true Hammond by blood, as well as looks. The boy had recently lost his father. To lose his newly discovered uncle, as well, a man who looked just like his father…what would that do to him? Zac ground out a curse, at the same time giving an ironic laugh when he had to jam his foot down hard on the brake. There was a gate ahead and he would have to stop to open it.

By the time he'd reached the other side of the gate and shut it behind him, the black moment was past and his mind was focused on Bushy Hill.

It was dinnertime before Zac came back. Rachel had already fed and bathed Mikey, wanting him in bed and out of the way early, before he could blab to his uncle that he was about to turn four. She needed time to think and decide what would be the best thing to do—to keep her embarrassing secret or tell Zac the truth.

Zac Hammond was not the kind of man she wanted as a father for Mikey. Aside from his dubious character, he would seldom be around. Not that he would want the responsibility of a child, anyway. Zac wasn't the type to take on responsibilities. He had his own life, his own world with his wild animals. That was how he liked it and would want to keep it.

And what would the truth do to Mikey? As an acknowledged father—a largely absent father figure—

Zac would be an unsuitable influence on the boy, un-settling him and putting wild, reckless ideas into his head. She wanted Mikey to grow up to be a steady, responsible adult, with a normal, settled home life and a family one day, not to be an aimless loner like Zac, without any ties or responsibilities or anyone to love and care about or to love and care about *him*.

Yet how could she lie to Zac outright if he asked the question? Would it be right to stay silent, now that Adrian was gone and not here to be hurt? But how *could* she tell Zac the truth? What emotional turmoil and disruption to their lives would it lead to? She would have to sleep on it first.

Zac looked a real mess when he walked in. Dirt had mingled with sweat, his naturally unruly hair was matted and more disheveled than ever, and his shirt was filthy. Yet something deep in the pit of her stomach stirred at the sight of him. He still looked breathtakingly sexy and strong and disturbingly virile.

That he could affect her in such a raw, basic way brought a sharpness to her voice. "You'd better clean yourself up before you tell me what you've been doing." *What you've been doing to* my *land.* "You can tell me over dinner. My head stockman, Vince, and his wife, Joanne, will be joining us." She'd heard Vince's Land Rover returning a while ago and had rushed out to meet it.

She often invited Vince and his new bride to the homestead to talk over station matters. If not to dinner, to drinks on the veranda, sometimes joined by Danny and whoever else was working at Yarrah Downs at the time.

"Can you wait for a cold beer until they come?" she asked Zac. "Or make do with some water for now?" How lucky that she'd asked Vince and Joanne for dinner tonight. Now she wouldn't have to be alone with Zac.

He grinned.

"Sure. Where's Mikey?"

"He's already in bed. He tired himself out."

"Reaction to all the excitement earlier in the day, hmm?" Zac's dirt-smudged lips curved in that roguish way he had—so unlike his more serious twin brother, and so like Mikey. So disturbingly like Mikey.

"Reaction to being scared to death, more like it," she heard herself snapping back, her nerves suddenly on edge. "Are you going to go and clean up or not?"

"Yes, ma'am." He loped off, still grinning.

While she was waiting for him to come back, Vince and Joanne arrived, freshened up after their day spent checking the water bores. They lived in the head stockman's cottage on the far side of the yards, past the communal bungalow Danny shared with any other stockmen working on the property.

Vince and his wife were both hardworking, rough-diamond types. Vince was short and muscular, with a shock of sandy hair normally hidden beneath a battered Akubra hat. Joanne, as strong and tough-talking as a man, had inherited her wiry strength from her stockman father and her dusky beauty from her Aboriginal mother. She pulled her weight with the men out on the station and acted as cook on musters.

Rachel often worried that Joanne knew more about

station life than she did. She had a feeling that Vince thought so, too, that he still thought of his new boss as a cosseted, wet-behind-the-ears "townie."

"Is there something wrong?" she asked the moment she saw their faces.

Vince's mouth was dragged down in a grimace. "We found that one o' the bores—Boomerang Bore—has been tampered with and put out of action, maybe wrecked beyond repair. We'll have to bring in a contractor quickly to fix it. If it *can* be fixed. We might need to sink a new bore."

Rachel's heart sank. How on earth would she be able to afford to fix it, let alone pay for a new bore if they needed it? It would cost a fortune! Yet she had to find a way. Without water her cattle would die.

Tampered with, Vince had said. "Who would do such a thing?" she cried. Her eyes clouded. Someone who didn't want a woman running Yarrah Downs? Someone who wanted to demoralize her and drive her out?

The person most likely to benefit if she did leave was Vince. He'd made no secret of the fact that he wanted to manage a cattle station one day, now he was a married man with responsibilities. He must think this a perfect opportunity—the city-bred widow, left alone with a young child, finding herself unable to cope with the demands of a busy cattle station. Putting a few obstacles in her way might drive her out all the faster.

Rachel felt a wave of despair. How could she keep Yarrah Downs running if she couldn't even trust her own head stockman?

"Beats me." Vince shook his sandy head. There was no sign of guilt on his sun-weathered face, no sliding away of his crinkled gaze, but then, Vince seldom showed any emotion. "Young hooligans? One of our neighbors, keen to buy up your land if you decide to sell? Or maybe some contractor who doesn't like dealing with a female station owner."

"Is that how *you* feel, Vince?" she asked bluntly.

"No, of course not." But his ready denial wasn't convincing. He didn't expect her to stay. Not for the long term. Not when he knew her own father was doing his best to persuade her to sell and move back to town. Nobody expected her to stay. And Zac, she suspected, shared the sentiment.

As if her thoughts had conjured him up, Zac appeared, his hair still damp from his shower, his clean shirt splashed with droplets of water. In place of the boots he'd been wearing earlier was an old pair of sneakers. He looked perfectly at home already in his brother's house.

She sensed Vince stiffen at the sight of him, heard Joanne's quick intake of breath and said as coolly as she could, "I don't suppose you've met Adrian's twin brother, Zac Hammond? Zac, this is my head stockman, Vince Morgan. And this is his wife, Joanne."

"G'day, Zac." Vince stretched out a freckled hand. By the mystified look on his face, it was clear that Adrian had never mentioned a brother to his head stockman, or if he had, he'd kept quiet about Zac being an identical twin.

As Zac clasped the outstretched hand, Rachel could almost read Vince's mind: *couldn't have been much brotherly love between 'em if the boss never mentioned having a twin brother.* And how right he would be!

To explain her brother-in-law's long absence from Australia, she gave a sketchy background. "Zac's a wildlife photographer. He works in remote parts of the world, taking photographs for geographic and wildlife publications and making documentaries. He's come back to Australia to do an assignment here."

Was that a flicker of relief in Vince's eyes? Or merely a flicker of interest? Had he wondered for a second if Zac had come back to take over the family property, dashing any hopes he might have had of running the station himself?

"Good to meet you, Vince. Joanne." Zac was all smoothness and charm as he turned to Vince's bride, who gave one of her rare smiles and thrust out her own hand. Rachel had the strangest feeling, as Zac's hand closed over Joanne's, that it was her own hand being clasped in that warm, firm grasp, and she had to swallow and look away.

"How about a cold beer?" she asked, and receiving nods all round—Joanne always joined the men in a beer—she hastened back to the kitchen. She normally had a weak gin-and-tonic herself, but tonight she chose mineral water, knowing they'd be having wine with dinner. With Zac around, she needed to keep her wits about her.

Over drinks she asked Zac about his inspection of Bushy Hill, half dreading his answer. She wasn't sure how much damage Adrian had done before his fatal accident. For Mikey's sake she'd kept well away from the hill in the past month.

Zac pursed his lips. "I guess it could have been worse. Most of the hill's been untouched, luckily, but quite a bit of native scrub and a few trees along the lower slopes are gone, exposing the bare earth to the elements. I'd advise putting in some drains before the rains come, or you could face an erosion problem."

Drains? How much would *they* cost? Rachel took a quick gulp of her drink, wishing she *had* chosen something stronger.

"We can only hope the wildlife hasn't been disturbed too much." Zac's jaw gritted as he said it. "My other worry is that the dam below the hill is almost empty. We'll need to bring in a water tanker to refill it, or the wildlife and the cattle out there will run out of water. Or be in danger of getting trapped in the mud if the dam dries up any more."

Rachel's spirits nose-dived. Drains...trucking in water...repairing or maybe even replacing the damaged bore... All tasks that would cost money she simply didn't have.

She felt Zac's eyes on her face and knew he'd sensed her dismay. Now he, too, would assume the property was too much for her, just as everyone else did.

"Don't worry, Rachel. I said I'd fix my brother's mess and I will. I need to fly to Brisbane in the morning to see about the plane and to bring some more fuel in, but first I'll arrange for a water tanker to come and for a truck to deliver the plastic pipes and gravel I'll need for Bushy Hill. I'll work on that when I get back tomorrow. Then I'll scatter some seeds around for eventual regrowth when the rains come.''

As her lips parted in protest—how dared he take charge and leave her to face the bill?—he drawled, ''My expense, naturally. Bushy Hill's always been my special interest. Please don't deny me this one thing I can do for Yarrah Downs, Rachel.''

She hesitated, frowning, wondering about his motives. If she allowed him to sink money into the property, she would be obligated to him. He might even expect to become a partner, an equal, if mostly absent partner, with the right to make decisions—decisions she might not agree with.

''No strings attached,'' Zac said, as if he'd read her mind. ''It's the least I can do for my family.''

Well, that made sense. He hadn't done too much for his family in the past. And she and Mikey were the only family he had now that Adrian had gone.

''Well, if you insist,'' she said, trying not to sound too grateful. *No strings,* he'd said. No, of course not. Zac Hammond didn't believe in strings or getting involved in other people's lives. Let him do something for his family in the short time he was here. He'd be gone soon, anyway. ''I have more pressing matters to deal with,'' she said with a shrug.

''The damaged bore should be our first priority,'' Vince said, drawing a quick frown from her. It was precisely what she'd been thinking herself. Did he have to treat her like an ignorant female who needed to have decisions made for her?

She stifled her indignation. He was only trying to help. It was his job to help her. ''I'll call the contractor in the morning,'' she said, wondering how in the world she was going to pay for it. The bank had refused further credit. ''It'll cost a bit to repair. If we need to sink a new bore, we…we might have to leave it for a while. It'll cost an arm and a leg. Meantime, we'll just have to move those cattle to another paddock.'' Water for the cattle was vital.

''If you need to sink a new bore,'' Zac said, ''I'll see to it. You can pay me back when you can, Rachel.''

She recoiled. To accept that kind of help from Zac would really put her in his debt. He'd have a real hold over her. She'd be in his power. He'd love that.

''I don't—''

''A *loan,* Rachel. Just like you'd get from a bank. Only, I won't be charging interest or putting any pressure on you to pay me back until you're ready.''

But maybe you'd put pressure on me to pay you back in some other way. She felt her legs go weak. Whatever his motive, he wasn't making the offer out of the goodness of his heart. Zac Hammond *had* no heart, according to Adrian.

Besides, she had to stand on her own two feet. Somehow. She'd never asked or expected her father to help her, and to accept help from Zac would be the first step to admitting defeat.

''How did the bore get damaged?'' Zac turned to Vince as if the matter was settled.

Vince stuck his thumbs in his leather belt. ''Looks like someone dropped a metal tool down the shaft and it's jammed up the works. As if we don't have enough problems. We badly need a few *extra* bores, but I guess we'll have to forget about gettin' those till Boomerang Bore's fixed.''

He shook his head, making Rachel feel personally responsible. *Everything's falling apart since Adrian's death,* he might as well have added.

''Any idea who's responsible?'' Zac asked.

Vince shrugged. ''Whoever did it covered up his tracks too well. Could've been anybody.'' He looked hard at Zac before raising his beer glass and taking a long swig.

Rachel's heart stopped. Surely Vince didn't suspect *Zac?* He'd only arrived today. *Unless he'd come back earlier and kept out of sight until now.* She felt as if she'd been punched in the stomach. Could Zac have flown into a nearby airstrip, borrowed a vehicle and made nightly excursions onto the property from there? Who would know his way around Yarrah Downs better than Zac, who'd been brought up here?

Her gaze speared his, but he was examining his beer glass with frowning intent, as if pondering the question. *Or avoiding her eye?*

Or did he simply agree with everyone else and believe she wasn't up to running the place? Her head stockman certainly had his doubts.

''Yeah, pity the damage to Boomerang Bore has wrecked any chance of puttin' in brand new bores,'' Vince muttered, his brooding gaze still fixed to Zac's face.

Rachel's arm jerked, spilling the drink in her hand. Was Vince now trying to inveigle her brother-in-law into paying for a couple of *additional* bores?

Her eyes flashed a warning—to Zac as much as to

Vince. "Try having more faith in me, Vince," she snapped, and switched the subject. "What's Danny been doing today? Where is he?"

Vince took a gulp of his beer. "He's been out checking the fences. He's not back yet, but he's been in contact by radio."

They all used radios because cell phones had poor reception out here. Only Danny possessed one of the powerful new satellite phones. His parents had given it to him, to keep in touch with them.

"There's more bad news, I'm afraid," Vince muttered. "Or it could've been."

Her brow knitted. "What do you mean?" she asked, her spirits dipping.

"Danny found a fence post knocked down near Michael's Gap and a big hole in the fence. He assumed it had been done by cattle until he found that someone had deliberately cut the fence wires."

Oh, no. A silent moan rose in her throat. "Cut them? Deliberately?" Who was doing this to her?

"Luckily Danny thinks only a few cattle have wandered into the next paddock—where there's no water, by the way, so it shouldn't be too hard to round them up in the morning. Jo and I'll go and help him. In the meantime he's staying up there till he's mended the fence."

Rachel felt a suffocating sensation; she was possibly in the same room as the culprit. She jumped up, needing to get away. Needing to take some long, deep breaths before facing them again. "I'll serve up the dinner," she said, and fled the room.

* * *

"Been here long, Vince?" Zac asked over Rachel's tasty beef-curry-and-rice meal.

"About five years," Vince said. "I started a few weeks before Adrian and Rachel got married. The previous bloke had retired. Too old for the job."

"You mean Bazza?" Zac's gray eyes glinted suddenly. "But you kept the old bloke on, I hope, as an odd-job man or something?" He frowned. "Where is he, by the way? I haven't seen him around."

"He left. I dunno where he went." Vince looked at Rachel, who shook her head. Adrian had never mentioned anyone called Bazza.

Zac's brow plunged, his powerful frame swelling in his chair, which suddenly seemed too small for him. "Bazza would never have left Yarrah Downs voluntarily. He would have had to have been kicked out. This has been his home for as long as I can remember."

"Well, he must have decided to go somewhere else," Vince muttered, "because he was gone by the time I came."

Zac didn't pursue the subject, but by his brooding silence, Rachel knew he was blaming his twin brother again. It wasn't until Vince and Joanne left soon after the meal that Zac brought it up again, following her out to the kitchen with a stack of dirty plates. It had obviously been eating at him for the past hour or so.

"Did Adrian ever talk about Bazza, Rachel? Mention where he went? He had no family but us. Hell, I didn't think even my brother would stoop to throwing Bazza out."

Her chin jutted out. Was Zac going to blame her husband for everything? "I know nothing about him. Adrian just told me the previous head stockman was too old for the job and had left. He never told me where he'd gone, if he even knew."

She switched on the hot-water tap, squirted detergent into the sink, and started washing the glasses. "If he was old, maybe he was sick and wanted to live in a town. He could even have died by now. I'm sure Adrian was doing what he thought best for Bazza. For Yarrah Downs."

Zac gave a snort, at the same time grabbing a tea towel to help her. "Bazza was a tough old codger. He was never sick a day in his life. Adrian always had it in for him. But I never thought his dislike had gone this deep. To deliberately turf the old bloke out. My father told Bazza he'd always have a home here, even when he was no longer able to work."

"We can't afford to keep people on out of charity. We're barely surviving ourselves." She winced, wishing she hadn't let that last bit slip out. She didn't want Zac knowing just how bad things were. She plunged a dirty plate into the sudsy water and swished it with a cloth.

Zac slid a hand onto her shoulder, his fingers spreading over the bare skin at her nape. The touch was so unexpected that she flinched. Or maybe she was flinching at the memory the warmth and texture of his fingers evoked.

With a quirk of his lip, Zac let his hand drop away. "I know it must be difficult, Rachel, especially when there's some vandal out there trying to make things even more difficult for you. But Bazza was one of the family. He belongs here. And a promise is a promise.''

Something in his voice got through to her. Zac really cared about this Bazza character. It wasn't just pique at what his brother had done to an old family retainer.

''Look, I'll try to find out what happened to him,'' she promised. ''And if he *is* still alive and didn't want to leave Yarrah Downs, I'll see if I can persuade him to come back. But he'll have to be able to work for his keep. Do odd jobs, at least.''

''Thank you, Rachel. But I reckon he'd be more likely to listen to me than to…Adrian's widow. He and my brother barely tolerated each other. I'll make some inquiries myself. I want to catch up with the neighbors, anyway.''

Oh, he did, did he? Why? To let them know the prodigal brother was back in Australia, about to work on an assignment here, before he flitted off again? She gave a jerk of her shoulder. ''Well, if you like. If you feel you have the time.''

How long would it take Zac to find the old man? Hours? *Days?* She felt herself trembling. Zac was becoming far too involved in the affairs of Yarrah Downs, when the place was her responsibility, not his. He'd asked to stay for a night or two, but it was becoming alarmingly obvious that he would never do all he wanted to do in a couple of days, or even a week.

It seemed inevitable now that he would be here for Mikey's birthday.

"Mind if I leave you to finish up here?" She threw down the dishcloth. She had to get away from him. She had to do that thinking *now*. "I have some book-keeping to catch up on." Adrian had always insisted on doing the books, and it had taken her a while to sort out the mess he'd left. Records not kept, bills not paid. He'd been no bookkeeper. Yet he'd never asked for her help or accepted it.

"My pleasure, Rachel." The amused glint in Zac's silver-gray eyes unsettled her even more as she made her escape. He knew he still affected her. But did he know in what way, or how deeply? Did he wonder just what, precisely, she felt for him? Attraction? Repulsion? Desire? Suspicion?

Did she know herself?

Chapter Three

Zac rose with the misty dawn, expecting to be gone from the house before anyone else appeared, but he found Rachel already up, making coffee in the kitchen. The aroma was seductive. Rachel, damn it, looked seductive, too, even this early in the day.

Before she turned to face him, his gaze drank in the sexy curve of her hips, her suntanned slenderness, the single golden braid snaking down her back. He wanted to tear it free and feel the silky strands slide through his fingers.

He curbed the urge and damped down other more-basic urges that had plagued him since his arrival. "Coffee smells good. Mind if I join you?"

She swung round, her lips parting. No lipstick, he noted, but her mouth was pink and lush enough without it. No makeup of any kind, nothing to hide the faint shadows under her blue eyes, as if she hadn't slept well or long enough. Had she been lying awake worrying about the problems she faced at Yarrah Downs?

Or had she been thinking about him, and cursing his return, because it brought back the humiliation of five years ago?

He wondered what else it brought back, if anything. That was what he had to find out.

But right now wasn't the time. "Another hot day coming up." He glanced out the window. "Still no sign of rain, unfortunately."

"No." She seemed distracted. "Here." She handed him a cup of coffee and poured another for herself, turning her back on him to do it. "I wasn't expecting you up this early. We normally have breakfast later, after I've done a few chores and everyone's gone off for the day. But a coffee first up is a must. Can I get you something to eat before I go out? Or will you get it yourself?"

She was talking too quickly, sounding breathless. He affected her all right. But he still wasn't sure if it was in the way he hoped.

"Just the coffee, thanks. I want to leave for Brisbane early, so I can be back in time to put that drainage system in—assuming the stuff I ordered gets delivered today, as promised. Mind if I take your pickup to Bushy Hill this afternoon? Your *ute*, I should say. Guess I've been away from Australia too long."

Her eyes flickered for the briefest second. "No problem. I'll get Danny to help you," she added, as if to reassert her authority. "They should have the cattle rounded up by then." She took a sip of her coffee, then dashed some milk into it—maybe to cool it down so she could drink it more quickly and rush off, away from *him.*

"I'm going to Roma to do some shopping, dropping Mikey off at a friend's place on the way," she said. "My friend Amy's married to a doctor in Roma and has a son Mikey's age."

"You go all the way down to Roma for your supplies? You don't use the general store at Booroora? It's much closer."

"I want to buy some things you can't find at Booroora." She didn't look at him, rushing on as if afraid he was going to quiz her further. "Amy's invited me to lunch afterward, so I might not be home when you get back from Brisbane. I'll leave some lunch for you."

"Thanks." He gave her a smile—a bland smile, carefully devoid of any roguishness—wondering why she was so much on edge. Was it him? Because he was outstaying his welcome? Because she felt things for him she didn't want to feel?

"Danny and I might be late back tonight," he said, taking a long sip of his coffee, "so you go ahead and have dinner. I'll grab something when I get back if I need it. I'm used to fending for myself."

"I know." She gulped down the rest of her coffee and made a beeline for the door, as if she couldn't get away from him fast enough. "I must catch Vince and Danny before they go. See you when I see you, Zac."

"See you, Rachel. Uh, Mikey's still in bed, is he?"

She paused at the door. "Mikey? No, he's always up early. I said he could run on ahead with Buster and watch Vince and the others saddling up the horses. Sorry, I must fly. They'll be ready to go."

Zac plunked down his coffee mug. "I'll come, too, and say g'day before I fly out." But she was gone.

He followed regardless.

Rachel heard Zac behind her but didn't wait for him to catch up. She didn't want to be alone with him. She'd had a really rotten night and simply didn't feel up to it.

She'd come to no real solution during the night, despite hours of tossing, agonizing about what to do. In the end, in sheer exhaustion, she'd given up, deciding to play it by ear and just see what happened. Zac might not *want* to know, even if he had suspicions about Mikey. He might even assume she didn't know the truth herself, since as far as he knew, both he and his brother had made love to her at around the same time.

Made love? She almost tripped over her own feet, her lip curling in hot-cheeked rejection. There'd been no love involved in that frenzied, impassioned tumble on the veranda.

And yet…and yet…

She almost groaned aloud, remembering how she'd cried out her love for the man she'd thought was her husband in the final cataclysmic moment of release, and how she'd felt more real soul-wrenching love in those mind-shattering few seconds than she'd ever felt before—or, to her endless shame, since.

I love you. I love you with all my heart, she remembered crying out, and in the months and years since, whenever she'd made love to her husband, it had always been the memory of Zac and that one unforgettable night that had fired her responses and haunted her dreams, possibly because her husband's clumsy, rushed lovemaking—always in the dark and always in bed, never on a moonlit veranda floor—had become less frequent as time went on, leaving her frustrated and dissatisfied.

But she had disappointed Adrian, too, by not having another child. Unless he'd known in his heart that the problem was his and had let it eat into him, making him feel worthless and impotent.

"Uncle Zac!"

Her son's screech of joy brought her back to earth with a sickening thud. When had Mikey ever greeted Adrian like that? As the boy hurled himself at Zac, she could only watch in despair. It was as if Mikey loved Zac already, as she had loved him, too, on that one memorable occasion, when her heart and soul had soared to heights never reached before or since.

Was this to be her punishment? Knowing that the love she'd felt for Zac that night, before she'd realized her shameful mistake, could never come to anything, because it had never really existed?

Late that afternoon, as she swung her Land Cruiser into the dusty road winding back to the homestead through the parched paddocks of Yarrah Downs, she saw that Zac's plane was back. There was no sign of her old utility truck—her *ute,* as he'd remembered to call it—when she reached the yard, so he and Danny must be still up at Bushy Hill.

Buster bowled up to greet them as she brought the big four-wheel-drive to a halt behind the house. She gave Mikey a bag of provisions to carry in and picked up some shiny black plastic bags herself. She'd bought Mikey's birthday presents in Roma while he was out of the way with his young playmate Josh, and she wanted to sneak them into the house without him seeing what she'd bought.

Through necessity they were modest gifts—a dinosaur picture book, a new shirt and knee-length shorts, a toy racing car in his favorite red and a bright yellow water pistol, which had seemed less bloodthirsty than a toy gun.

She'd also secretly made Mikey a monster mask out of papier-mâché, painting it in vivid colors at night while he was asleep. Monsters and dinosaurs were his latest craze.

She wondered if she would ever be able to afford to give her son a playground slide or a fancy two-wheeler bike or anything more ambitious. His grandfather had given him a shiny new tricycle for his last birthday, but Mikey had just about outgrown it.

At the thought of her father her mouth drooped. In two days' time he would be flying up here for Mikey's birthday and no doubt would give his grandson another lavish gift to show up her own failings in that area.

He'd be sure to point out that both she and Mikey

could have whatever their hearts desired if only they'd come back to Sydney. And he'd probably say it in front of Zac, who'd no doubt support her father and urge her to sell in favor of an easier, more comfortable life back in the city.

She'd have no one on her side but Mikey, who loved it here and relished the open, free-and-easy outback life, despite the heat and the dust and the flies. But Mikey, as her father would remind her, had never known life in the city. There were plenty of attractions there that her son was missing out on—movie theatres, science museums, sporting arenas, playgrounds, zoos—attractions that a young boy, he'd argue, ought to be exposed to.

He'd often begged her to let Mikey go and stay with him in Sydney, or for her to come, too, for a short break, but so far she'd resisted, using the excuse that her son was too young and that she was too busy. Her father was a powerful man, and she was half-afraid that once he had them back in town, he would find some way to keep them there.

Since Adrian's death, her father had been more single-minded than ever about her coming back home and reclaiming her heritage—Barrington's—and helping him run it, as he'd trained her to do. Having lost her mother last year—the one person who had seemed to understand her need for independence and a different kind of life—her father now had no one to curb his burning ambition for his only daughter and grandson.

She would just have to stay strong—though with this debilitating drought and these costly, destructive setbacks and everyone seeming to be against her, it was becoming more difficult by the day.

Zac and Danny didn't return until well after dark, by which time she'd had dinner and put Mikey to bed.

She was doing some mending, patching a pair of Mikey's jeans, when Zac breezed in, looking even grubbier and dustier than he had the evening before. And just as disturbingly, powerfully male.

"All done," he reported, his eyes gleaming with satisfaction. "And sooner than expected. When dusk fell, I decided to take a closer look at the wildlife. Took some photographs while I was about it. Depending how they turn out, I might include them in my Australian assignment."

She gave a wry smile. Of course. Zac would never forget his own work or forget to take his cameras with him, no matter how pressing his family's problems were.

"Mind if I grab a beer?" He was already heading toward the fridge. Yeah, he felt at home here, all right. "I'm too filthy to sit down inside. How about joining me out on the veranda, Rachel, so I can bring you up-to-date? I'll clean up later."

Was he afraid she'd scuttle off to bed if he went to have a shower now?

"Sure." She'd feel less vulnerable if he stayed in his present grimy state. It was hardly conducive to getting close. She felt nervous enough already at the thought of being out on the veranda alone with Zac. Too many disturbing memories swirled around out there. But it *would* be cooler outside.

She led the way, conscious of a tingling from her feet all the way up her legs as she emerged from the house and trod edgily over the timber boards that had felt the weight of their writhing bodies five years ago.

As Zac stepped out behind her, his dark head almost touching the overhead vines, he murmured, "I'd almost forgotten how perfect the evenings can be in Australia."

He inhaled deeply, drinking in the balmy air and the sweet scent of the roses in the garden below, mingled with the pungent scent of eucalyptus drifting in on the slight, warm breeze. "Clear skies, a nearly full moon and so many stars you could count them forever. No, don't switch on the lights. We won't need them."

As a frisson of alarm quivered through her, she stood hesitating, not sure she felt game enough to sit with Zac in the moonlit darkness. But at least she'd be able to hide her thoughts more easily. She sank into a wicker armchair, turning it toward the moon rather than facing Zac as he dropped into the chair opposite.

"So, you've finished laying your drains at Bushy Hill?" She kept her gaze fixed on the ghostly ball in the sky. The moon always had a soothing effect on her. In the garden below, noisy cicadas pierced the night air with their searing, monotonous chirps.

"Yeah—with Danny's help." Zac sounded so calm, so cool, as if unaffected by the scene of their shame. Was he as calm as he sounded? "Then we scattered some seeds around. Might as well try for some regrowth. I've arranged for a water tanker to come to fill the dam, but it mightn't be here for a day or two. Danny says the other dams are holding up, though only just. If it would only rain, I'd be a lot happier.''

He'd be happier! ''I think it's forgotten how to rain.'' She ran pensive eyes over the unbroken mass of stars. Not a cloud in the sky, let alone a rain cloud. Even nature was conspiring against her. ''Danny pulled his weight okay?'' she asked.

Her young jackaroo, a brash young science graduate from a wealthy Sydney family, could be a bit big for his boots at times, thinking himself above the menial tasks of an apprentice stockman and not always working as a team member, preferring to do jobs on his own. But he was intelligent and quick to learn, and he deserved the chance to gain some experience.

''Well, I had the feeling he thought it a bit pointless protecting a hill we don't make any practical use of, but he kept his thoughts to himself. He's obviously a bright kid who wants to get on. How long has he been here?''

''Not long. He turned up out of the blue, but with excellent references, about three weeks ago. Our previous jackaroo had moved on, so I took him on.'' She'd warned Danny she couldn't pay him much, but he'd assured her he was here to learn and to experience outback life, not to make money. ''I suppose he was curious about *you*?'' The question leaped out.

''He did want to know how I fit into the scheme of things.'' Zac's tone was sardonic.

She whipped her head round. ''I hope you told him

you're not staying. I don't want him starting to look on *you* as his boss. It's hard enough running this place without my authority being undermined.''

Zac's eyes, a dark gleam in the moonlit gloom, probed hers, making her glad the veranda lights weren't shining into her face. ''Have no fear of that, Rachel. I want to help you out, that's all—as any brother-in-law would. As I made clear to Danny.''

She wondered if he'd also mentioned to Danny how long he'd be staying. Another day? Another week?

''Well, thanks for what you did.'' Credit where it was due. ''You've no need to worry about Bushy Hill after you leave here, Zac. There'll never be a vineyard there. I'll see to that.''

A dark eyebrow rose at the words *after you leave here,* but all he said was, ''That's good. Thanks.''

Rachel raised her glass to her lips. She hadn't really wanted a drink, but to give herself something to hold on to, she'd poured herself a cold lemonade. The minute she finished it, she would excuse herself and go to bed. Being alone with Zac on a balmy moonlit night, especially out here on the veranda where they'd once shared such shocking intimacy, was far too unnerving.

It was becoming more hair-raising by the second. She could feel her skin prickling, her heartbeat going haywire under his shadowed gaze, while the air between them seemed to pulsate with electric tension.

''Were you happy with Adrian, Rachel?''

Her heart giving a thunderous bang, like cymbals

crashing in her chest. *Get a grip, girl. It's a perfectly natural question.*

She unlocked her throat, uttering the words she'd parroted countless times to her father. "Adrian was a wonderful husband. And a wonderful father." Did the words sound as hollow to Zac as they did to her? Yet they were basically true. He *had* been a wonderful husband and father in many ways, totally devoted to his wife and son and to Yarrah Downs. It was only as a lover that he—

Don't go there. Don't!

She was half-afraid Zac was going to persist and ask again, *But were you happy with him?* Instead, he drawled, "How did you two meet? When he wrote to let me know he was getting married, he told me you were a city girl. Adrian hated going to the city."

She gulped, willing her heart to settle down again. Some hope. "I was traveling in the outback at the time I met him. I was keen to see more of my own country."

She'd already traveled overseas, to Europe and America and parts of the far East, after plucking up the courage to tell her father she needed to "do my own thing" for a while. He'd insisted on her traveling first-class and at his expense, hoping, no doubt, that a few months of overseas travel would get the restlessness out of her system.

But it hadn't. On her return she'd felt the urge to explore her own country, to see another side of life, a more basic, down-to-earth side than her pampered life in the city and her five-star travels overseas, and she'd told him so, closing her ears to her father's arguments and entreaties. This time she'd used her own savings.

"I traveled around Australia by train and bus. I loved the outback—the Kimberleys, Ayers Rock, the Northern Territory, the wide-open spaces. Queensland was my last leg. There was a rodeo while I was at Longreach for a weekend. I met Adrian there, and…well, we just clicked."

He'd been so different from the polished, smooth-talking, money-mad city types she'd mixed with in the past. He was a genuine Aussie bloke, the strong, silent type, so deeply tanned and good-looking, so unassuming and down-to-earth, so unlike any other man she'd ever known, that she'd fallen quickly and hard, her romantic heart convinced she'd found the man of her dreams.

"He asked me to go to the Longreach bachelors-and-spinsters ball with him that night, and I did."

"And that was the start of it?"

"Yes. When he heard I'd never seen a cattle station, he invited me to Yarrah Downs the next day. I ended up staying for a week. He had his married housekeeper stay at the homestead while I was there to act as a chaperone. He was a perfect gentleman. I hadn't met too many of those before then."

Her mouth twisted a little. She couldn't image Zac Hammond ever being so gentlemanly as to consider a girl's reputation for five seconds, let alone keeping his hands off her for days on end, and certainly not for weeks, as it had been with Adrian.

"And did she? Chaperone you?" Zac seemed to find that amusing. Of course, he would.

She raised her chin. "Adrian had no need of a chaperone to act honorably." She'd admired his restraint at the time. All her previous boyfriends had tried to rush her into bed from the word go. "At the end of the week Adrian proposed marriage and I accepted."

In hindsight, she should have taken longer, made sure he *was* the man of her dreams. But then she would never have met Zac and had Mikey.

"Adrian insisted on going back to Sydney with me to tell my parents and to give me time to prepare for the wedding." She shivered, recalling her father's reaction, which had only made her more determined to get married as quickly as she could.

"My. I never knew my brother could be such a fast worker. Had he…kissed you by then? Behind the discreet back of the chaperone, of course."

She turned to face Zac, a withering glint in her eye. The last thing she needed was Zac Hammond's sarcastic barbs. "I wouldn't expect you to understand respectful, gentlemanly behavior. Of course he'd kissed me. He just hadn't ravished me."

It was the wrong thing to say. Like a red rag to a bull. "But did you ravish *him?*" Zac asked softly, a faint smile on his lips.

Her cheeks flamed. "Certainly not. I've never ravished anyone, except my own husband." *Or a man I thought was my husband.* She'd been too frantic with frustrated longing that night to notice or care about any differences. "I can see why you and your brother didn't get on," she snapped. "You have no idea of respect or morals or how to treat a woman."

He leaned forward, the wicker chair creaking under his weight. "If I'd been Adrian, my sweet, I wouldn't have been *able* to resist you. Which is what happened the last time I was here. I couldn't resist you. Simple as that. Just as you couldn't resist me, whether you knew who I was at the time or not!"

She sucked in a sharp breath and sprang to her feet, knocking over her glass. Zac's hand shot out, gripping her wrist, preventing her from running away. She gave an outraged yowl. "Let go of me!" His fingers felt like fire on her skin, searing her flesh like a branding iron.

"And I'm not sure you can resist me now," he murmured, alarming her even more by rising from his chair and towering over her, "even knowing I'm not your husband. But you don't *have* a husband now, do you, Rachel? There's just you and me."

Zac couldn't believe what he was saying. He hadn't intended to confront Rachel so soon, let alone like this! It was a gamble that could well wreck everything, but damn it, he had to know how she felt! It had been driving him crazy. *She* was driving him crazy.

He pulled her against him, sliding his other arm round her waist—not violently, but gently, seductively. "Tell me you don't feel anything, Rachel. Tell me you don't want to kiss me the way we kissed before."

Too late he remembered the dust and grime streaking his face and hair, the filthy state of his shirt and jeans. But he didn't intend to back away now, when he had her in his arms at last. If she rejected him, he could live with the regret later.

But *would* she reject him? The need to know was overpowering.

Rachel couldn't believe the sapping weakness she felt, the honeyed heat searing a path down her thighs. His warm breath was on her face, his firm sensual lips tantalizingly close. He smelt of native scrub and dust and sheer maleness. Why had she ever imagined she'd be safe from him, just because he was covered in grime? She'd never be safe from him. He'd been in her blood for the past five years!

She gave a yelp and struggled to free herself. "Let me go! I d-don't feel anything!"

"No? Then why are you trembling? Why is your body on fire? Why aren't your struggles more convincing?"

That did it. Zac knew it a second too late. He'd gone too far. This time she used all her strength, fighting him off and writhing out of his grasp. Being a lot stronger, he could have held on to her, but he backed off—for now.

Let her think about his warm breath on her face, his body burning into hers, while she was trying to sleep tonight. Let her think about the trembling response he'd felt in her, even as she'd struggled to free herself. It hadn't been horror or repulsion or fear he'd felt in her. She'd felt the same irresistible attraction she'd felt five years ago.

It gave him hope.

"Calm down, Rachel. I've let you go, see? I'm not even touching you. I was just making a point. Okay,

I was out of line. You don't feel anything, you've convinced me,'' he assured her, lying through his teeth. ''I'm sorry. You can sit down again.''

''What, after *that?* I don't think so. I'm going to bed.'' For good measure she stomped on his foot before flouncing away. It had little effect because he was still wearing his thick leather boots. But the message was plain enough.

Rachel was still trembling, still weak and hot and sweaty when she reached her room. Why did Zac have this drastic effect on her? Why hadn't she simply laughed at him and treated it as a joke? Why did she have to react like an outraged adolescent, showing him he only had to touch her to set her on fire?

She stormed into the bathroom that Adrian had built off the master bedroom and cursed Zac, because she knew she *would* lie awake, reliving the bone-melting response she'd felt in his arms, the burning need, the unwanted coil of heat snaking through her body, wishing she *had* let him kiss her, longing even now, to feel those hot sensuous lips on hers as she'd felt them once before and dreamed of ever since.

Why had she never felt this scorching need for her own husband, even in the romantic early days of their marriage? Why had Adrian never felt it for *her?* Yet he'd loved her, she'd never doubted that. He'd even proved it before he married her, by standing up to her father the way he had, resisting Hedley Barrington's contemptible efforts to buy him off and get him out of her life.

And she'd tried hard to love her husband in return,

for the qualities she could admire in him, quenching her growing sexual frustration in hard work and long, exhilarating horseback rides.

Adrian's reluctance to make love to her before their wedding night should have sounded warning bells. She'd put it down to old-fashioned respect and a quaint, gentlemanly restraint—the very things Zac would scoff at. But in hindsight, it might have been better if Adrian *had* made love to her before she'd committed her life to him. Maybe then, she would have *known* how it was going to be.

But she'd been in love—or at least thought herself in love. She would still have gone ahead and married her strong, silent, steadfast cattleman and willingly embraced her exciting new outback life, convincing herself that their lovemaking would improve over the weeks and months ahead, with more practice and deeper intimacy.

Only it hadn't improved, even after five months of marriage, and then Zac had come along, and for the remainder of her short-lived marriage to Adrian, she'd suffered the torment of knowing what she was missing out on.

Rachel squeezed her eyes shut.

And yet…just what had that electrifyingly intimate encounter with Zac meant, when it all boiled down? Nothing! What had happened between them five years ago had been unbridled sex, pure and simple. To read anything more into it was crazy.

She had to squash the lustful feelings she still had for Zac Hammond. They were purely physical and meant nothing, certainly not to him. He didn't care about her or any woman—not in the long term. He'd just been making a point tonight, he'd admitted it. That was the kind of man he was. How she hoped she *had* convinced him.

But had she convinced herself?

Zac went to bed with a smile on his lips. Rachel could fight it all she wanted, but she still felt something for him, just as he'd suspected—and hoped. Knowing that made it easier to back off—to wait, at least for the time being, although, damn it, the waiting was going to be hell. He could still feel the fiery heat of her body, still smell the subtle scent of her hair, still see the dilating pupils in the moonlit glow of her eyes, a sure sign of desire, even as she'd struggled against him.

It was torture! Torture and heaven, or the promise of heaven, at least.

He slid a hand over his pillow, imagining it was her hair spread across the smooth fabric. He buried his face in its softness and gave a muffled groan, trying to damp down the raging heat still firing his body. One day, he thought, it would be Rachel in his bed, not a pillow. One day.

Chapter Four

The next morning Rachel skipped her early-morning coffee and went straight to her outdoor chores with Mikey. She needed to take a few deep breaths of fresh air and wake herself up properly before facing Zac again.

Besides, she wanted to catch Vince and the others before they left for the Ten Mile to spend the day repairing the drafting yards.

The sky was a blinding golden-orange where the sun was rising over the distant hills, the few low wisps of cloud tinged a vivid vermilion. But they weren't rain clouds—that would be too much to hope for. It looked like another hot, depressingly dry day coming up.

She found Vince and Joanne already climbing into

Vince's four-wheel-drive. "Where's Danny?" she asked. "I thought he was going with you."

"Nah. Danny's gone to Brisbane for the day. It's a wonder you didn't hear his motorbike burning off real early this morning." Vince settled behind the wheel. "I gave him the day off."

"*You* gave him the day off? You didn't think to ask me first?" Irritation creased her brow. Another example of Vince assuming the role of boss!

"He only told me last night." Vince's gruff tone was defensive. "Today's his parents' silver wedding anniversary. They're flying up from Sydney to meet him at some posh hotel in Brisbane for dinner tonight. He said he'll be back tomorrow in time for Mikey's birthday lunch."

Mikey's eyes lit up. "D'ya reckon he'll buy me a birfday present in Bisbane?"

"He'll be busy with his family, Mikey." Rachel spoke rather sharply, having already warned her son not to expect presents from the station people, who seldom had a chance to go shopping. She didn't want Vince and Joanne to feel obliged to produce a present.

She turned back to Vince. "There'll be someone coming shortly to examine the damaged bore. If it can't be repaired, we'll have to sink a new one." Her heart dipped at the thought. She might be forced to accept Zac's offer of a loan. But she would make sure he knew it was just a loan. "I'll drive out there with him. I want to see the damage for myself. Maybe the fiend who did it left some clue behind."

Her gaze flicked over Vince's face. He and Joanne were the ones who'd discovered the damaged bore—

or that had been their story. Maybe they'd done more than just discover it.

"If you're hoping to find any telltale tracks or cigarette butts or anythin'," Vince drawled, "forget it. I've already looked."

Or already covered them up? Rachel kept her eyes on his face, but it showed more skepticism than guilt.

"Well, be seein' ya." Vince broke eye contact as he revved the engine. "Remember we'll be campin' out at the Ten Mile overnight so we can get the job finished in the mornin'. Be back before lunch."

"I'll be back in time to help you with the salads, Rachel," Joanne promised.

"Thanks, Jo."

As the Land Rover shot off, Mikey spun around with an excited whoop. "Uncle Zac!" He broke into a run, his small arms flung wide. "Will you take me for a ride, Uncle Zac? You promised!"

Rachel watched as her son threw himself into Zac's strong arms. Her eyes prickled. Such innocent trust. Such blind adoration. Such unconditional love. But was Zac worthy of the boy's trust? Adrian had never thought so, and being Zac's identical twin, he must have known Zac better than anyone.

And Adrian had had good reason not to trust his irresponsible brother—as she, his wife, knew only too well.

But didn't I play a crucial part in that unthinking betrayal?

She snapped off the humiliating thought, sighing deeply as she watched them, father and son together. It was easy enough to be a hero when you didn't have to sustain your hero status in the long term, day after day, month after month, year after year. When you didn't have to exert discipline and rules or think about constancy or stability or where the next dollar was coming from.

"Sure, I'll take you for a ride, Mikey. How about now, before breakfast? If it's okay with your mum." Zac shot her a look that defied her to deny her eager-eyed son. "We'll ride side by side. No leads."

"As long as you stay close to him," she said, a warning in her tone. "He's only a little boy, remember."

She could have bitten out her tongue when Mikey's mouth opened in immediate protest. "I'm not little! I'll be four tomorrow. Are you coming to my birfday, Uncle Zac?"

She stifled a silent moan. *Keep calm. Play it cool.*

"Zac might not be here at lunchtime tomorrow, Mikey." She kept her eyes on her son's face, not Zac's, afraid of what she might see in those piercing gray eyes. The quick calculation? The vital question? "Grandpa's coming for your birthday, remember, and your friend Joshua, but Zac might be too busy. Didn't you say you wanted to look for your old friend Bazza, Zac?"

She risked a glance at him, hoping her face reflected her concern for the old man rather than her fear of the truth about her son coming out. Not that Zac would bring it up now, in front of Mikey. Even he wouldn't be that crass.

"I was planning to start making some inquiries about him today after breakfast." Zac's easy drawl gave nothing away. If he had any suspicions, he wasn't showing them. "I wouldn't miss your birthday for anything, Mikey. I'll be here. If it's okay with your mum, that is."

"It's *my* birfday. *I'm* inviting you," said Mikey, before his mother could say otherwise. "Everyone's coming. You *have* to come, Uncle Zac. We're having a barbecue lunch. And a monster birfday cake, wif candles."

"Of course it's okay, Zac," she said, her light tone hiding her qualms.

Zac wasn't her only concern. She didn't relish the thought of her father rubbing shoulders with her brother-in-law and station hands and hearing about all the setbacks she'd been having lately. But she'd had to invite them all—Mikey had demanded it, and how could she have denied his wish? Birthdays were a big thing to a four-year-old, and he had few enough friends way out here.

She was glad her friend Amy was coming, too, with her son, Josh, Mikey's only friend of a comparable age within visiting distance. She'd wanted to make it a special day for her son, though out of necessity it would be a casual, relatively simple celebration.

At least, with so many people around and so much for her to do, her father would have little chance to nag her about returning to Sydney.

"You'll find Silver and Maverick in the home paddock." Her brisk tone belied her inner turmoil. "Mikey's already familiar with Silver, on a lead at least, and Maverick's good with strangers—and he won't spook Silver. You know where the saddles are?''

''I'll show you, Uncle Zac.'' Mikey dragged him away, flinging a last word over his shoulder at his mother. ''You can go and do what you have to do, Mummy. I'll be safe with Uncle Zac.''

Safe? With Zac Hammond, the reckless adventurer, the footloose loner, a man who'd never accepted responsibility in his life?

She watched them go, the tall, broad-shouldered man with the untidy mop of dark hair, and the small boy with the same confident stride and the same dark, unruly locks.

''I know you will,'' she whispered, gulping, recalling Zac's strong arms carrying Mikey down to safety from the top of the windmill. Of course he'd be safe with Zac.

Over a robust breakfast of fried eggs, homemade sausages and crisp bacon, Zac said between mouthfuls, ''Before I fly out to see if the neighbors know anything about Bazza, I'll take a few low swoops over the paddocks, just in case there's anything that shouldn't be there.''

Or any*one*, he meant. Rachel slid a look up at him. Would he offer to do that if he was the culprit himself?

He might if he's cunning enough and wants to put me off the scent. But in her heart of hearts, she didn't believe that Zac would stoop to such depths. Surely, if Zac wanted Yarrah Downs for himself, he would already have offered to buy her out.

On the other hand, maybe not. Maybe he just wanted to soften her up a bit first. There were ways of softening up a woman and wearing her down. A stolen kiss, a spot of sabotage, a shrewd reminder of the drought and the pressing need for water, a lavish offer of financial help—a loan, rather, that he knew she wouldn't be able to pay back in the foreseeable future.

She whisked the plates from the table and sought refuge at the sink, gulping in air through the open window—only, the air was already hot, windless and oppressive, hardly refreshing. Mikey, mercifully, hadn't stopped chattering since he'd come back from his ride with "Uncle Zac," so there'd been little need for her to make conversation over breakfast.

Thankfully, she hadn't yet found herself alone with Zac.

That was the moment she was dreading. Had Zac picked up on the date of Mikey's fourth birthday and done the math? Luckily Mikey had arrived nearly three weeks late, so his birth had been closer to ten months from conception rather than the telltale nine. Would that be enough to allay any suspicions?

"I'd better be running along." Zac scraped back his chair. "I'll also need to fly to Rockhampton." He didn't explain why, making her wonder, with an inexplicable dip of her spirits, if it was to discuss his Australian assignment and start getting it under way. "I'll pick up some beer for your barbecue while I'm there."

"Thanks," she said, without turning her head. He

must have noticed her beer supplies were running low and felt partially responsible.

"I'll be back before dark, but don't wait dinner for me. I'll grab something at one of the neighbors' if I'm hungry."

How confident he sounded that the neighbors would welcome him back with open arms. Would they even remember him?

"You're sure you're happy about having Bazza back, Rachel?" he asked as if he'd picked up some vibes from her tense stance. "Assuming I can find him and he wants to come back."

Now she did flick a look around. "I meant what I said," she answered rather sharply. Did he think she was as incapable of keeping a promise as her husband had been? She inhaled a deep breath, feeling disloyal at the thought. Adrian could have had a perfectly sound reason for letting Bazza go. Bazza himself might have wanted to leave.

"Can I go up in the plane with Uncle Zac, Mummy?" Mikey was looking up at her with his big silver-gray eyes. Zac's eyes.

"Uncle Zac's going to be gone all day, Mikey. I thought you wanted to come out to Boomerang Bore with me and then help me prepare for your birthday lunch—decorate your birthday cake and set up the birthday table on the veranda, with some fun decorations. And we must start blowing up the balloons."

"Yeah!" Mikey cried, and started shoveling cereal into his mouth, anxious to finish his breakfast and start the ball rolling. Zac grinned, and slipped out while he had the chance.

* * *

Whew. Looking down from the Cessna, Zac had never seen Yarrah Downs so parched and dry, the once-lush paddocks so brown and lifeless they were almost bald. The creek that wound through the property had completely dried up and the dams were dangerously low. Even the hardy Santa Gertrudis cattle, normally a healthy cherry-red, looked lethargic and out of condition. According to Vince there'd been no summer rains at all and virtually no winter or spring rain prior to that. And now autumn was heading the same way.

He swooped low, checking cattle and fences, circling bores and water holes, scanning clumps of trees for anything out of the ordinary, anything at all suspicious—but all the while his mind was elsewhere.

Mikey would be four years old tomorrow.

Adrian, he mused, had never been much of a stud. He'd shown little interest in girls or sex when they were growing up, never boasted of any conquests, even though he'd talked of having a wife and children "one day."

He wondered why Rachel and Adrian hadn't had another child in all the years since Mikey was born. If his brother had been incapable of having children...

Was it possible? Could those few moments of wild, unthinking passion have produced a child? But she'd assured him before he left Yarrah Downs on that traumatic night that there was no possibility of any "consequences." She'd been adamant that it was a safe time of the month—unless she'd been trying to convince herself as much as she was him.

His heartbeat thudded in his ears, seeming even louder than the drone of the Cessna's engine. Could Mikey be *his* son? If so it was clear that Rachel had no intention of telling him, or she would have told him already, surely. She'd had enough chances.

But then, she didn't want him in her life, or in Mikey's.

Or *thought* she didn't.

Well, it's a whole new ball game now, sweetheart, he thought, nearly slicing the top off a tall ghost gum with his plane's left wing.

It's time to up the ante, my love. High time.

Rachel had dinner with Mikey earlier than usual, willing Zac not to come home until they'd finished and she'd put Mikey to bed.

She blew out a relieved sigh as she left her son's room and settled down to catch up on her book work, reaching up to switch on the reading lamp before flicking on her aging computer. Zac would have to come home soon—it was already starting to get dark. Unless he planned to stay overnight at one of the neighbors' and fly back in the morning, in better light.

She mentally crossed her fingers, knowing she was a coward, but wanting to delay the fateful moment. Of course, he might never ask the question. He might not even *care*. But did that make it right to keep on withholding the truth from him?

She stared into the computer for a while, then leaned back, raking her fingers through her hair, unraveling her already loosened braid. How could she possibly concentrate on depressing facts and figures that didn't add up while all *this* was churning around in her head?

She turned her face upward to feel the breeze from the overhead fan. Heck, it was hot, even with the fan. It had been sweltering out at Boomerang Bore earlier today, and the news had been bad. The bore was wrecked, as she'd feared, and a new one was already in the process of being sunk.

And of course she'd found no incriminating evidence at the bore, no clue to the vindictive lowlife who'd tampered with it, just as Vince had warned.

Yet *someone* was to blame.

She banged her fist down on the table in frustration, and the computer screen went black. At the same time the reading lamp went out, the electric fan above her stopped whirring, and the plugged-in radio playing soft music fell silent. The only sound was the drone of a light plane overhead.

She groaned. Great! The power had gone out, and Zac had arrived home. All she needed now was the roof to fall in!

She turned to the window. Darkness had closed in outside, and the moon was hidden by thick cloud that seemed to have rolled in from nowhere. How on earth was Zac going to see to land? With no power, she couldn't switch on any lights in the yards.

The only thing she could think of was to jump into the big Land Cruiser, drive down to the airstrip and shine her headlights at him. Would she have time?

Where the heck had she put her flashlight? She knocked over her chair as she jumped up, then fumbled her way across the room, banging into furniture. Did it always get dark this darned quickly?

The kitchen! There was a flashlight in the kitchen. She bumped into a table and swore, rubbing her hip. But as her eyes became accustomed to the darkness, she could see vague shapes.

Suddenly she heard the drone of the plane's engine stop. She held her breath, her chest tightening, waiting in dread for the sound of a crash. But there was no crash, not even an audible thud. Zac had landed safely in the dark.

As she crossed the kitchen, she heard a spattering on the roof. Rain! It was a sound she was desperate to hear. She hoped it wasn't just a passing shower. *Oh, please, let it rain for days! For weeks!*

"Mummy!" The plaintive cry came from Mikey's bedroom. She knocked a bottle off the shelf as she felt around for the flashlight she kept there. Finding it was like grabbing a lifeline. She switched it on— and nothing happened. Brilliant! The battery was dead!

"Coming, Mikey!" It took her a few more minutes to find a candle and a box of matches. When she had it alight, she headed for her son's bedroom, being careful not to run in case it blew out. She could hear rain drumming on the iron roof, but just as she reached Mikey's room, it stopped. *Oh, please, don't stop now.* Was that short downpour all they were going to get?

"Mummy, my light's gone out." Since his father's accident, Mikey had been having the occasional nightmare, and she'd bought him a night-light in the shape of a horse to keep by his bedside for comfort.

"It's all right, pet. The power went off. It'll probably come back on in a minute." But she didn't hold out much hope. They were miles from anywhere, and the emergency services weren't exactly just around the corner. She paused to wonder why the power had gone off, but Mikey was her first concern.

"I'll see if I can find some batteries, darling, and then you can have the flashlight." A candle by his bedside wouldn't be safe.

As she found batteries and settled him down again, she heard footsteps approaching the back door. Checking that her son was asleep, she plucked the flashlight from his fingers, put it down beside his bed and headed back to the kitchen, clasping the candle. She wasn't sure if the air was making the candle flicker, or her shaking hands.

She met Zac as he strode in, shaking droplets of water from his hair.

"Why is everything dark? What's going on?" His voice was a fractious growl. It must have been hairy landing on a darkened runway at night with no lights to guide him. And being caught in that short-lived downpour wouldn't have helped his mood. He sounded worn-out, as well.

Well, that was good, she decided. He'd want to crash into bed early. He wouldn't feel like hanging around talking. *Asking questions.*

"Sorry if it was difficult landing in the dark. The power suddenly went out—just before the rain." Her voice sounded equally testy. It wasn't *her* fault there were no lights or that he'd left it so late coming home. "I'll have to ring the electric-repair people. And they'd better come out soon or everything in the freezer will thaw, and the food in the fridge and the cool room will spoil and we'll all melt without any fans."

And what about Mikey's birthday lunch tomorrow? Luckily the outdoor barbecue ran on bottled propane, so they could still cook the meat. And she'd baked Mikey's birthday cake already—a monster cake with a ghoulish face, as he'd wanted. The rest of the food would be cold stuff—salads and savories that she could prepare in the morning and keep in the fridge, even if it had lost most of its chill.

"What about the old two-stroke generator we used to keep in the shed?" Zac asked. "It would keep the fridge and the fan going, at least."

She sighed and shook her head. "I noticed it was missing the other day—Adrian must have lent it to a neighbor who forgot to return it. I—I haven't chased it up because I've had other things to think about. The power supply's normally reliable." Another black mark against her, she thought.

"Well, just as well we're having people here for a barbecue tomorrow. You'd better cook up all the meat in your fridge—the stuff in the freezer should last a bit longer. I've dumped some cartons of beer in the cool room. It should stay cold for a while."

"I wonder how it happened—the power going off, I mean." She glanced up at him.

In the glimmer of the candlelight, the lines and shadows of his face were accentuated, making him look tougher, harsher, even vaguely threatening. Certainly threatening to her fragile state of mind. "There's no wind, no storm, no lightning about. Only some rain that seems to have passed already." Her voice wobbled. "Why would the power suddenly go off?"

"Did you hear a bang?" he asked. "I mean, like an explosion?"

"I don't think so." Would the thump of her fist on the desk and the drone of Zac's plane have muffled the sound of a bang?

"If it had been the transformer blowing, you would have heard it—it's not that far from the house. I'll take a look around in the morning. In the meantime, you'd better call for someone to come out. But don't be surprised if they can't come for a day or two."

She growled a curse. With no fans, no ice-cold drinks, how could she hide this latest setback from her father tomorrow? He'd relish having more fuel to add to his perpetual refrain. *You can't stay on out here, love. Outback life's too difficult for a woman on her own. Come home where you and my grandson can be safe and pampered and comfortable. And cool.*

She scowled. "Have you eaten?" she asked Zac.

"Yeah. That's why I'm late. The last place I visited—you might know the Grangers, they've a sheep farm near Roma—really turned on the hospitality."

She raised her brows. So even after all these years, the neighboring landowners wanted to swamp the prodigal twin brother with hospitality. Yet none of them had ever mentioned him—at least, not in front of her. They must have known Adrian and his brother didn't get on.

"Did you find Bazza?" she asked, remembering the old man.

"Not yet. But I know where he is. I'll need a four-wheel-drive to reach him. He's living in an old stone hut at an unused cattle station next door to the Grangers' sheep farm. He's become a real hermit, they tell me, just wanting to be left alone."

The harsh lines of his face deepened in the candle's glow. "Since he ran his motorbike into a ditch and wrecked it last year, Bazza never even goes into town for supplies. He lives off the land. Grows his own vegetables, has a few fruit trees and gets water from an old well. Otherwise he relies on bush tucker—berries, leaves, worms and stuff."

"Worms!" She pulled a face. "Poor Bazza."

"Bazza knows how to survive in the bush. But he's an old man now, and his accident's left him with a limp. Heaven help him if he gets sick."

"But if he's happy living like that…"

"I'll convince him he'll be happier back here." Zac's jaw clenched. "And I'll do it as soon as I can."

"You'll go and find him tomorrow?" Would he put Bazza ahead of Mikey's birthday lunch? Her eyes clouded. If he did, after promising Mikey he'd be there, then he was as irresponsible as Adrian had painted him.

"You think I'd miss Mikey's birthday?" His gray eyes pierced hers in the candle's warmth. "I don't think you realize, Rachel, how much your son means

to me. Or how much I've come to mean to Mikey…
already.''

She swallowed. ''You…you feel that strongly
about him?''

''Yes, I do. He's the closest thing I have—or will
possibly ever have—to a son. We share the same flesh
and blood.'' His voice was quiet, but every soft word
held her riveted. ''He already feels like a part of me.
I couldn't feel any closer to him if he *was* my own
son.''

Her heart stopped. She felt the room tilt. *If he was
my own son.* How could she let it lie there? Even
though he probably only meant…

Oh, dear heaven, what *did* he mean? What did he
know? Had he guessed? Was this the moment to tell
him, to confirm it?

Suddenly the candle was whisked from her grasp,
its flame wobbling as Zac spun it halfway across the
kitchen table. In the same fluid movement his strong
hands grasped her arms. His face, in deep shadow
now, was so close she could feel his hot breath on
her cheek.

''You seem a trifle unsteady, Rachel. Are you all
right?'' The soft purr of his voice held a mocking
undertone. His broad-shouldered frame, a dark shape
looming over her in the candle's flickering glow,
seemed about to swamp her.

''Of c-course I'm all right.'' *Oh sure, just listen to
that pathetic croak!* ''Why wouldn't I be?''

''You tell me.'' He swung her around so that the
candle on the table lit her face. ''Why is it, Rachel,
that whenever your son's name is mentioned, or his

birthday is mentioned, you react like a startled rabbit?''

Did she? And she thought she'd covered up so well! "I...I don't." Oh, heck, this was pitiful! What was the point in denying it any longer or playing these silly games? Adrian was gone—nothing could hurt him now. Only Mikey could be hurt if Zac turned his back on him.

But Zac did care for Mikey. He'd just said so, and he'd shown it already. Surely he wouldn't do anything to harm him?

It would be wrong, unfair to Zac, to hide the truth any longer. He deserved to know. He had a right to know. Surely they could discuss this like mature adults?

Amazingly, Zac didn't press her for an answer, changing tack before she could form the words she needed to say. ''There's always been a special rapport between you and me, Rachel.'' His tone had gentled. ''You felt it five years ago, even though you might not have realized it at the time. I've felt it again since I've been back—an instant connection, a chemical pull or whatever you like to call it, an overwhelming need...''

She gave a faint whimper. Oh yes, she felt it all right—the burning weakness, the helpless longing, the urgency to connect with him, mouth to mouth, body to body, until they were spinning out of control, soaring to even more rapturous heights than the first time.

But afterward...how would she feel afterward? After the rapture had died away? Didn't he realize it wasn't enough? She needed more. More than just a fleeting sexual connection, powerful and wonderful as it might be while it lasted. With Zac, she must remember, nothing lasted.

"Don't keep denying how you feel, Rachel, because it's as indisputable as I'm standing here. I only have to touch you..."

She felt his warm hands run up her bare arms, and the answer was in the trembling weakness he must be feeling under his fingers.

"I've been dreaming of you for the past five years," he admitted in a soft growl, "but in all that time I was trying not to, hating myself for what I did to you, what I did to my brother, to your marriage. It's the only time in my life I've wanted someone with such an overpowering need, such mindless passion, that I ended up losing all control."

She shook in his arms. She understood perfectly what he meant, because she'd felt the same way. She still did, hard as she was fighting it. The fact that he was accepting all the blame himself and not reminding her of her own shameless part in the affair made his admission even more earthshaking. As if he was baring his *soul* to her.

Only, it had nothing to do with his soul, and to believe it did was pitifully foolish and naive. It was still only sex, animal lust, a helpless, uncontrollable passion. It wasn't love.

At least, not for him.

She moaned and turned away. Was *that* what was happening to her? Was this what falling in love felt like? This agony of need and despair, this uncertainty, this bone-weakening, mind-shattering yearning? A yearning for something she wanted desperately but knew would never happen, would never last, because nothing lasted with Zac.

"Think about it, Rachel." Gentle fingers cupped her chin, easing her around to face him. "Think about what you feel, what I feel…" His lips touched hers, lingering for just a second, just long enough for her to taste their warmth, their promise. But his hands were already falling away, his head drawing back, removing the lips she ached to feel devouring hers, and longed to feel all over her body as she'd felt once before and dreamed of so many times since.

"And think about what Mikey feels," Zac murmured. "And what he needs. A father."

Her startled gaze flew to his. But like a panther in the night, he'd already moved away, only his words remaining, hovering in the oppressive air. As silently as the flickering candle on the table, he vanished into the gloom.

Chapter Five

Zac thrashed about in his bed in a lather of sweat, burning with frustration, wondering how he'd found the strength to walk away from her. But if he hadn't, he would have lost control again, and it was vital he stay in control this time, at least until he was sure Rachel was ready, or until *she* took control—or lost control and begged him to take her where he ached and burned to take her.

He groaned into his pillow. Was *this* staying in control? This scalding heat in his loins, this sweat pouring from his body, this rasping breath in his throat? He could still taste her, could still smell the subtle fragrance of her skin, her hair, could still feel her in his arms…

Heaven help him, if he didn't take a cold shower right now, this minute, he damn well *would* lose control.

Rachel felt a warm body land on hers and reluctantly roused herself from her lustful dream.

"Mummy, wake up! It's morning!"

Still half-asleep, she reached out to hug the small body sprawled on top of her, wanting to feel her son's very real warmth, even though it wasn't the same sort of warmth she'd been dreaming about a second ago.

Her son's usually soft cheeks felt strange and hard as she tried to kiss him, and smelled vaguely of paint. She forced open sleep-drugged eyes, and the early-morning glow revealed a grisly, vividly colored monster mask, with gaping eyes and bared teeth.

"My goodness, a monster!" she cried. She'd put the mask at the end of Mikey's bed last night while he was asleep, to surprise him on waking, keeping aside his other gifts for later. "Please don't eat me, Mr. Monster," she begged, secretly pleased with the result of her efforts.

Mikey giggled. "It's me, Mikey," he said, lifting the mask to reveal his grinning face. "I won't eat you, Mummy."

"Mikey!" She feigned surprise. "Happy birthday, darling!" She curled her arms around him again and kissed him—on his rosy cheek this time. "I thought you were a real monster!"

Mikey giggled again, then wriggled out of her arms. He had no time for this soppy stuff. Not today. A boy's fourth birthday was far more important. He rolled off the bed and stood facing his mother, hiding his face again behind the gruesome mask. "Have you got any more presents for me, Mummy?" He eyed her hopefully through the round eye holes.

"Hmm…let me get dressed and we'll see if we can find any."

"Can I look for them?" Tearing off the mask again, Mikey swiveled around, his eager gaze sweeping the room, looking for brightly wrapped parcels. "Turn on the light, Mummy, so we can see better."

Rachel tried the lightswitch, knowing it was a vain hope. As expected, nothing happened. "The power's still off," she said. It meant she wouldn't be able to use the electric kettle for her early-morning coffee. She'd have to light the wood stove and boil up a pot on that. And there'd be no fan to keep the kitchen cool, either. The air was already sultry and close after the rain in the night.

"Don't worry, I can see all right." Mikey's mind was still on his birthday presents, his small, pajama-clad body wiggling with the effort to remain patient.

"Well, then, you could look in my wardrobe." She didn't have to tell him twice, watching with a smile as he made a dive for the corner where she'd hidden his gifts. Mikey ripped the wrappings asunder and pounced on his shiny red sports car, his dinosaur picture book, his new shorts and matching top and the bright yellow water pistol.

"Wow! Oh, boy! Wow!" He seemed delighted with each one.

She said again, "Happy birthday, Mikey," and

headed for the bathroom, leaving him to take a closer look at her modest offerings.

Mikey seemed disappointed later when he ran ahead of her to the kitchen wearing his monster mask and found that Zac wasn't there. There were no sounds coming from his room, either.

"You'll see him at breakfast, Mikey." Her heart gave a flutter at the thought. "And remember, he'll be here with everyone else for your birthday lunch. Have some orange juice for now, then you can go out and try out your new water pistol on Buster. He'll think it a great game if you shoot water into his mouth. You could fill his water bowl, as well. But don't use too much water. We mustn't waste it." Wasting water during a drought was a criminal offense.

Two minutes later the back door slammed behind her boisterous son. She smiled and shook her head. Perhaps now she would have a few moments of peace.

She removed the monster mask from the kitchen table and spread out a clean cloth. As she reached up to a cupboard for the breakfast bowls, a shrill scream from Mikey and a series of sharp, high-pitched barks from Buster abruptly shattered her short-lived peace.

She rushed outside.

"Mummy, Mummy, there's a snake!" Standing motionless, as he'd been taught to do with snakes, Mikey was pointing at the water tap. Buster, still barking, had taken up a protective stance in front of his young master.

"I see it. Don't move, Mikey." A long, russet-colored snake was wriggling away from the water bowl underneath, trying to make its escape, mercifully not heading toward her son or the yapping dog. "I'll grab the spade!"

She shot into the laundry room where she kept one for just such an emergency, snatching it up and leaping after the slithering snake. Mulga snakes were highly venomous, and she didn't want one hiding under the house or hanging around in her backyard, threatening her precious son.

She moved with lightning speed, gripping the rusty spade with firm hands and raising it in readiness. A couple of swift hard blows and it was all over.

"Can I hit the snake, too, Mummy?" Mikey begged. "Vince says—"

"You're too little to take on snakes just yet, Mikey." She wondered if Zac would agree with what she'd done. Would he have let the snake go?

But if she'd let it escape, it could have slithered under the house and she'd never know when it was going to come out, maybe slipping *into* the house next time in its search for water. She'd found a snake in her bathtub once.

"You can fill Buster's water bowl—quickly—then go back inside," she told him. "Take a look at your dinosaur book while I check the yard." *And dispose of the snake.* "I'll be with you in a minute."

Zac didn't turn up for breakfast, but having noticed by then that Maverick was missing from the home paddock, Rachel assumed he'd gone out already to inspect the power line. Vince and Joanne would still be up at the drafting yards, and Danny wouldn't be back from Brisbane until lunchtime.

"You can help me blow up some more balloons,"

she told Mikey to take his mind off his uncle Zac. As for herself, she had a hundred other things to do before lunchtime. Hopefully, they would take *her* mind off Zac, too.

Rachel was hard at work chopping up tomatoes, onions and green peppers for a salad when Zac finally strode in, his dark hair as untamed as ever, his bush shirt partly unbuttoned, drawing her eye to a sexy V of bronzed chest, his skintight jeans accentuating the strong thighs underneath. The usual heat coiled in her belly.

Mikey, sprawled on the floor with his toy sports car, jumped up and hurtled across the room, thankfully diverting Zac's attention so that she was able to observe him with his son. This was the first time Zac had seen Mikey since learning the truth about him. Or *guessing* the truth.

"Uncle Zac, look what Mummy gave me for my birfday." Mikey paraded around in his smart new shorts and matching top, which he'd changed into after breakfast.

"And this—" he scooped up the toy car from the floor "—and a water pistol and a dinosaur book and a monster mask." He looked up at Zac expectantly, but Zac's hands were empty, and he made no mention of a present.

"Well, you're a lucky boy, that's for sure." Zac's mouth stretched in an eye-crinkling smile, which any onlooker, Rachel reflected with a gulp, might have called a father's indulgent smile. "Happy birthday, mate. Four years old. Are you too big now to give your old…uncle Zac a hug?"

Rachel's breath caught. She'd have sworn he'd been about to say *your old man,* but had changed it at the last moment. Had he deliberately made the slip for her benefit, to let her know that he *knew?*

She watched with wary eyes as Mikey threw himself into Zac's arms, to be swept up and whirled into the air, round and round, making the delighted boy shriek with laughter.

There was a strong bond between them, no doubt about that—perhaps an even stronger bond now that Zac had guessed the truth. But she hoped he would have the sense not to say anything to Mikey before she did. *If* she did.

She resumed her chopping, bowing her head to hide any visible yearning in her eyes. Things might have been different if she and Zac had been a couple living together, or getting married and intending to bond together as a family with Mikey, but that wasn't the situation. Zac was a footloose adventurer, a rolling stone, forever on the move. And besides, he didn't love her.

He wanted her, desired her, maybe even blazed with the need for her, but that wasn't love. Love was being unable to live without someone, wanting to share everything with the other person, heart, body and soul. Wanting to be together forever.

A tremor shook her. Was she in love with Zac? Had love grown from the secret helpless yearning she'd felt from the moment he'd first kissed her five years ago? Even after the shock of realizing who he really was, she'd known in her heart that she would never feel with any other man what *he'd* made her feel, that it was more than carnal, out-of-control lust she felt for him, more than a powerful sexual need culminating in a rapturous physical satisfaction.

Racked with shame and guilt, she'd stifled her painful secret all these years and tried to be a good and loving wife to her husband, knowing her hidden craving for Zac could never become a reality.

But she had no husband now and Zac had come back into her life; it was no longer possible to deny the feelings she'd buried and now felt springing to life again. Even though she knew the kind of man Zac was—the here-today-gone-tomorrow type—the more she saw of him, the stronger her feelings grew, despite her knowing so little about him or his reasons for being here—other than wanting her in his bed. *And maybe wanting Yarrah Downs if she put it up for sale.*

The squealing and laughter stopped as Zac put Mikey down, keeping hold of him until the boy had regained his balance—a caring gesture, Rachel thought, for a man whose own brother had constantly portrayed as thoughtless and uncaring.

''Why don't you go out into the yard with Buster, Mikey,'' Zac suggested, ''and see if there's anyone coming. I'm expecting a visitor.''

Rachel blinked. He was? ''Bazza's coming?'' she asked as Mikey raced out the door, as usual banging it behind him. Had Zac arranged the old man's homecoming already? But the Grangers' property was miles away, and Zac had taken Maverick out this morning, not her four-wheel-drive. To have ridden all that way and back on horseback... No, he couldn't have done it.

Zac shook his head. "I didn't go looking for Bazza this morning—that'll take more time. I went out to inspect the power line."

So he *had* been checking the line. Maybe his expected visitor was the electrician, coming early to fix it. Miracles occasionally happened. "Well?" she asked, noting the tightening of his mouth with misgiving. "Did you find anything?"

"The power line's been cut. Someone came onto the property, climbed one of the old timber power poles and deliberately snipped the wire, cutting off your power, Rachel. Unfortunately any tracks have been wiped out by that brief downpour we had overnight."

Rachel leaned on the table for support. Yet again someone had coldly, deliberately targeted Yarrah Downs, which meant they'd targeted *her*.

She felt Zac's hand on her bare arm, and for once she didn't react, didn't register any feeling, other than a vague feeling of comfort. She was too numb, too shocked. Who was doing these horrible things? Would they make a personal attack on *her* next? Or on Mikey?

A fierce, protective rage surged up inside her. If anyone tried to harm a hair of Mikey's head... She gripped the knife in her hand.

At the same time a sickening suspicion surfaced. Maybe they'd tried already. Maybe they'd deliberately planted that venomous mulga snake in her yard...

No, they wouldn't. They couldn't. Get a grip, Rachel. Snakes often come out in the dry weather.

But the power line… She swallowed. Someone had deliberately cut that.

Zac had been landing his plane when the power went off. It would have happened instantly, the moment the power line was cut. She trembled…in relief. At least it wasn't Zac trying to break her spirit and drive her out. But in her heart she'd never believed it was.

"I'll find him, Rachel." Zac's face was as hard as his tone. "I'll track him down and deal with the fiend, before he decides to target *you* next, or puts you and my son in real danger."

His son! Her gaze flew to his, her knees almost crumbling beneath her. So it was out in the open at last. It was a relief, in a way. "Please don't say anything to Mikey," she pleaded. "Not…not yet."

The hand on her arm applied gentle pressure. "Of course I won't—or not until the time is right," he drawled, giving her due warning that it was going to happen sometime. He didn't ask how she could be certain that he was the father and not Adrian. Maybe he'd known his brother even better than she had. They were identical twins, after all.

"But you might have confided in me, Rachel…earlier." His tone was gently chiding. "You could have trusted me."

"Could I? After what you—" She stopped, gulping, all too conscious of her own guilt five years ago. Zac at least had *tried* to tell her who he was that night, even urging her to "steady on," but she'd been too frantic with longing to listen, silencing him with her lips, thinking he was Adrian trying to fob her off again, pleading tiredness after his long trip or any excuse to avoid another failure in the bedroom.

But what had happened between Zac and her that night wasn't the only reason she'd found it so hard to trust her brother-in-law. Adrian had painted Zac as irresponsible, selfish and untrustworthy, an uncaring man who walked alone and preferred it that way. Hardly a man to put your faith in or want to confide in.

"After what I did to my brother that night?" Zac finished for her, his brow quirking. "I thought I'd explained how it happened, Rachel, how I've never lost control like that with anyone but you. I thought you were ready to forgive me in light of the circumstances and your own…equally ardent participation at the time."

Her body slumped. So he hadn't forgotten how she'd thrown herself at him on that fraught moonlit night.

And how could she ever forget, either? Her blatantly sexual greeting, her wild abandon, her careless waving aside of caution, despite Zac's attempts to set her straight. And worse, the way she'd blithely disregarded any differences in the sexual prowess of the man who'd arrived on her doorstep that night and the husband she'd come to know, thinking *she'd* inspired this new incredible passion in her husband because he'd been missing her, or because she'd boldly taken the initiative for once.

Only, the man she'd seduced hadn't been her husband, as she'd realized in horror the moment she'd come down from the rapturous heights he'd taken her to and her dazed mind had started working again, forcibly bringing back the words Zac had been trying to tell her before she'd silenced him with her lips, too hungry for passion to listen. *I'm Zac. You do realize...*

She trembled, remembering how she'd lashed out at Zac to cover her own shame and humiliation. But they were both equally guilty of betrayal. How could she go on letting Zac shoulder all the blame?

"I don't blame you, Zac," she said, valiantly meeting his eyes. "It just happened. As you said."

"Maybe it was meant to happen," he murmured. "Maybe you and I were destined to come together."

Her heart jolted. Would he speak of destiny if all he felt for her was sexual need? "What do you mean?" she whispered. "Isn't that a bit melodramatic? Talking of destiny? You'll be going away again soon."

"Wrong. I'm staying. I don't intend to budge from here while you and Mikey are in possible danger. I'm staying for as long as you need me, Rachel. You might not think you need anyone, but you do. Our son needs me, too. I can help you—and give you moral support. We'll fight this together—the drought and this lowlife vandal who's been causing you so much trouble."

He lifted his hand and stroked her cheek, giving her the overwhelming urge to bury her face in the warmth of his palm. "I'd like to think you might *want* me to stay, that you might want me yourself, Rachel, as much as your body has shown it wants me, needs me…''

She shivered under the sensuous brush of his fingers. ''But your Australian assignment…''

''I've put it on hold. Indefinitely. I want to help you get Yarrah Downs back on its feet, Rachel. Help you physically, not just financially. I want us all to get to know one another better, for you to know you can rely on me.''

As her lips parted, Zac gently sealed them again with his fingers. ''I'm well-off, Rachel. I can afford to help my family. I can make sure your cattle have adequate water by sinking more bores, in addition to the one we're replacing, and I can use my plane to muster cattle, check the fences and make sure the property's safe and secure. I intend to track down this creep who's been doing his evil best to drive you out.''

His eyes gleamed with steely purpose. ''And old Bazza's just the guy to help us. This latest attempt to crush your spirit will give me a good excuse to entice Bazza back here without him losing face. We need someone who can watch over you and Mikey during the day and help you check out anything suspicious while the rest of us are away.''

Rachel's mind was still reeling from what he'd said a second earlier. He intended to *stay?* And his *family,* he'd said, as if he thought of the three of them as a family now, a family he wanted to know better and be a part of.

But he'd been quick to switch the subject back to his old friend Bazza, away from any talk of the future.

Maybe he was afraid she might probe too deeply, ask for more than he was prepared to give. Well, she didn't intend to make *that* mistake.

"Maybe it's Bazza himself doing these things to us." She dragged out the unpalatable possibility. "Maybe, if he didn't leave here voluntarily, if Adrian gave him no choice, he's getting his revenge."

Zac shook his head. "Bazza doesn't have a malicious bone in his body. And since he wrecked his bike, he's had no transport. Anyway, he'd never be able to shinny up a power pole at his age, with his bad leg. Are you sure Vince and Joanne were both camping out at the Ten Mile last night?"

"Well, as far as I know. And Danny's in the clear. He was in Brisbane overnight with his parents. He won't be back until at least lunchtime." She glanced at her watch and frowned. "Vince and Joanne should be back by now. Jo said she'd help me with the salads."

"Can I help?"

"I thought you were expecting a visitor."

"I can lend a hand while we're waiting. Oh, sorry, Rachel, I think I hear the van now."

Van? Mystified, she followed him outside, in time to see a cream-colored van and a horse trailer pull up in the yard. Mikey was trailing alongside, waving his arms.

"Mummy! Mummy, look!" He veered toward them. "I think Grandpa's sent me a horse for my birfday!"

She opened her mouth and snapped it shut. Why in heaven's name would her father give Mikey a horse? He must know that a horse of his very own would only make his grandson more determined to stay at Yarrah Downs. Could this mean her father had finally given up trying to drag them back to the city?

"This is *my* birthday present to you, Mikey." Zac spoke up from behind. "A pony of your very own. From your uncle Zac."

Rachel's head jerked round. "*You* bought Mikey a horse?"

"Not a horse, a pony. Just the right size for a four-year-old. Far safer and easier to manage than a full-size horse." He strode forward to help the driver unload his son's birthday present.

Mikey jumped up and down. "My own pony! Wow!"

Rachel watched dazedly as they lured the pony from the trailer. It was a lovely-looking animal, a pie-bald black-and-white pony with the sweetest face and warm brown eyes. How in the world had Zac managed to find a pony at such short notice?

Was that why he'd flown to Rockhampton yesterday? There were horse auctions and pony clubs there. When Zac decided to do something, as she ought to know by now, he didn't waste any time.

"He's beautiful!" Mikey cried, hurrying forward to pat the pony, who calmly stood still for him, as if used to children.

"Happy birthday, Mikey." Zac put a hand on his son's shoulder. "His name's Rocky. He belonged to another little boy who grew too big for him. Rocky's always had a good, loving home, and he needs to be well looked after in his new home."

"I'll look after him," Mikey promised. "Hello, Rocky. Hello, fella. I'm Mikey. I'm gonna look after you real good. Wow! My very own pony!"

"You can keep him in the training paddock for now," Rachel said. "He might like to be close to you for a while, rather than out with the other horses. At least until he's used to you and is familiar with his new home."

"I'll see to it," said Zac. "You go and finish what you were doing, Rachel." He glanced around. "Ah, here's Vince's Land Rover now, so you'll have Joanne to lend you a hand. I'll look after Mikey and the pony. I bought Rocky's saddle, as well, so I can give Mikey a ride now, if he wants one."

Mikey gave a squawk. "I do! Come on, Uncle Zac!"

"Thanks, Zac." She smiled from father to son, wondering pensively how long this new, family-minded, home-loving side of her adventurous brother-in-law would last. Until he'd tracked down the vandal, and the challenge and excitement of the chase was over? Knowing Zac, he'd most likely equate it to tracking down a wild animal.

Or would he stay around as he'd vowed he would, until he'd helped her put Yarrah Downs firmly back on its feet? Or until it rained heavily enough to end the drought and he felt he could leave with a clear conscience, knowing his duty to his family was done until his next whirlwind visit home—whenever that might be?

Or until he'd slaked his desire for her, which he swore had been tormenting him for the past five years, and which she, a widow now, was finally free to respond to?

She trembled as she turned back to the house. Would Zac's desire for her rapidly burn itself out once he'd quenched the fires he claimed had been raging in him all these years? Would his itchy feet and his urge for adventure and brilliant wildlife photographs be stronger than his hunger for *her?*

She pressed her hands to her lips. How would she survive a blazing, short-lived affair with Zac Hammond, feeling the way she did about him? Wouldn't it be wiser, safer, less soul-destroying, to keep him at arms' length?

Chapter Six

Rachel glanced up as Joanne rushed in, full of apologies. "Sorry we're late, Rachel. We found a pregnant cow lying in one of the paddocks. The poor thing was having trouble giving birth…"

Rachel felt a quiver of foreboding, expecting, with her bad luck lately, to hear that they'd lost both cow and newborn calf. So many of their cows had been weakened by the drought. A few had already died.

"We stayed with her to make sure nothing went wrong." Jo gave a quick grin. "Don't worry, she gave birth to a healthy female. They're both in real good shape." She glanced up at the kitchen ceiling. "Has your electric fan konked out? It's so hot in here!"

Rachel's flare of relief turned to a sigh. "We had

a power failure last night and the power's still off. Zac checked it out this morning and found that some-one cut the power line.''

''You're kidding!'' Joanne seemed genuinely shocked. ''First the bore, then the damaged fence, now this. Someone must be sneaking into the property at night, some hooligan with nothing better to do. Or some goon with a grudge against us.''

Rachel was grateful for the *us*. It meant Joanne was thinking of them all as a team, not singling out the new female owner of Yarrah Downs.

Joanne flicked a look round. ''I can hear a plane. Sounds like your father's snazzy jet.''

Oh, great. Her father was early. ''I'd better go and meet him.'' She made little effort to hide the resig-nation in her voice. ''I'll grab Mikey on the way. Mind slicing up these bread rolls and buttering them, Jo? Everything else is pretty well done.''

''Oh, heck, is it? Sorry, Rachel.''

''It's not your fault you were late—you were help-ing out, and I appreciate it.'' Rachel flashed her a smile as she left the kitchen in search of Mikey.

She didn't have far to look. He was still riding around the training yard on Rocky, his small frame perched cockily in the saddle, with Zac looking on, shouting instructions. Buster was circling the pony at a discreet distance, as if to make sure this strange new animal behaved itself and did nothing to threaten his young master.

''Grandpa's here,'' Mikey called when he saw his mother. ''Can I ride down to meet him, Mummy?''

''I guess so,'' she said, and looked up to meet

Zac's quizzical gaze. Was he hoping she'd invite him along, too, as Mikey's uncle?

Her skin prickled at the prospect of her father coming face-to-face with her late husband's mirror image—he'd had no prior warning of Zac's existence. He would wonder why she'd never mentioned Zac, and might jump to all kinds of wild conclusions if she didn't prime him first.

"Thanks for looking after Mikey, Zac," she said, striding past him to catch up with her son. Realizing how dismissive she sounded, she softened her tone to toss back over her shoulder, "Would you mind setting up a bar near the outdoor barbecue under those gum trees by the shed? And seeing to the drinks when everyone arrives?"

"Leave it to me." His own tone was sardonic, as if he'd guessed what she'd been thinking. Those sharp gray eyes had a habit of seeing far more than she wanted them to.

Her father, a heavyset man with a thick mane of silver-white hair, had already emerged from his state-of-the-art Citation jet. Unlike most wealthy company chiefs, he insisted on flying solo on private flights, shunning copilots and bodyguards.

She raised her hand as he trudged toward her through the scorched grass, his bearlike arms holding a bulky, gift-wrapped object. Shiny handlebars protruded from the wrapping—a dead giveaway.

Mikey, still perched on Rocky, gave a hoot of delight. "Grandpa! Is that my birfday present?"

Hedley Barrington's hard, handsome face broke

into a smile—the indulgent smile he reserved solely for his grandson. It had been a long time since Rachel had seen it directed at her. "Yes, my boy, it is. You can unwrap it at your birthday lunch." *Where everyone could witness his generosity?* "Happy birthday, Mikey. Good morning, Rachel."

"G'day, Dad."

"Look, Grandpa, I got a pony for my birfday!"

Hedley's heavy-browed eyes zeroed in on Mikey's mount, registering the pony for the first time. His smile vanished. "You bought your son a *pony?*" Disbelieving eyes speared Rachel. "A four year-old-child?"

Along with disbelief was patent displeasure, Rachel noted. Her father would hate to see his grandson getting too attached to a pony. Ponies didn't belong in cities.

"Mummy didn't give me Rocky. Uncle Zac did." In his shrill high voice, Mikey set his grandfather right.

"Uncle Zac?" The heavy glare deepened. "You've a new stockman, Rachel? Who gives ponies for presents and has become familiar enough for your son to call *uncle?*"

"Zac *is* Mikey's uncle, Dad." Rachel outwardly kept her calm, though her insides were jumping. Just the thought of Zac was unsettling. "He's Adrian's twin brother. His *identical* twin brother. He's staying with us for a—"

"I didn't even know Adrian *had* a brother. You've never mentioned it. There was no twin brother at your wedding. Or at Adrian's funeral."

Rachel felt her cheeks warm. "Zac and Adrian didn't...they were never close. Zac's been working overseas for years. He's a wildlife photographer. His last assignment was in Zaire."

"But now he's come back." The sharp blue eyes below the heavy brows grew thoughtful. Calculating. "He wants to reclaim the family property, does he, now that his brother is dead? I hope you're not going to stand in his way, Rachel."

"He's just come back to pay his respects, not to buy me out." Damn! Why was her voice shaking? Because she'd wondered the same thing? Wondered if the urge to reclaim his old home was indeed Zac's hidden agenda, and if his interest in her was little more than a clever smokescreen, a ploy to lower her defenses and make her more willing to sell to him?

She thought of Zac's kisses, his passionate avowals, his genuine concern and obvious feeling for Mikey, and she sighed at her doubts, trembling at her own helpless feelings for him. Was it possible now that Zac knew Mikey was his son, he'd moved beyond his original ambition and now wanted to possess all three of them—Yarrah Downs, herself and Mikey?

But this was *Zac Hammond* she was talking about. He'd never want to settle down and stay put in one place. Not permanently.

"Zac's a photographer, not a cattleman." She spoke flatly, keeping her expression masked, her voice as steady as she could. "But he *has* offered to stay here at Yarrah Downs for a while...to give us a helping hand." It wouldn't hurt to let her father know that she had some family support, that she wasn't on her own.

"You need help?" Her father pounced on the admission. "You've always told me you can manage on your own."

"I *can* manage, but…" She stopped. How could she tell him about the willful damage and other demoralizing setbacks she'd suffered lately? It would only make things worse, giving her father a perfect excuse to pressure her into selling and going back to Sydney. He would insist that it wasn't safe for her or his grandson to stay, that anything could happen next.

Her father, already suspicious of her brother-in-law's motives, might even suspect Zac himself of inflicting that malicious damage on her, to scare her into selling more quickly, at a bargain price.

But the culprit wasn't Zac; she knew it wasn't. And before her father left here later today, she'd have to convince him that Zac was her protector, not her adversary. Then maybe her father would back off and leave her alone.

"Dad, why don't you give Mikey his present now?" she said, switching his attention to his grandson, who'd begun to wiggle impatiently in the saddle. "He can hardly take his eyes off it, and it must be getting heavy for you." She turned to her son without waiting for an answer. "Here, Mikey, let me help you down. I'll look after Rocky for you."

It did the trick. Her father said no more about Zac, standing by while his grandson ripped the glossy wrapping from his new bike.

"A two-wheeler! Wow!" *Wow* was fast becoming Mikey's favorite word.

His grandfather beamed at the boy's delighted reaction. "It has trainer wheels, see?" He pointed them out. "When you're bigger, you can learn how to ride without them."

"Uncle Zac'll teach me," Mikey said with his usual blithe confidence in Zac. "He'll teach me in no time. Then I won't need twainer wheels."

"You just be careful," his grandfather warned. "This Uncle Zac of yours sounds rather reckless and irresponsible. He doesn't seem to realize how young you are. Ponies and two-wheeler bikes without training wheels can cause nasty accidents…"

Shades of Adrian, Rachel thought with a wry smile. If they'd had their way, her father and her husband would have wrapped Mikey in cotton wool.

You can be too cautious, she recalled Zac telling her. *It can make you vulnerable.* She thought of the windmill incident and gave a rueful shake of her head. Just as well Mikey had a mother who could steer him on a sensible, moderate course, between the two extremes.

The roar of a motorbike startled Rocky, causing the pony to throw back his head, almost jerking the reins from her grasp. It took a minute for her to get him under control again.

"Danny!" With a frown she signaled for the young jackaroo to stop, which he did, wheeling his motorbike round and pulling up in a swirl of dust. "You're scaring Mikey's new pony. Must you ride so fast and rev up so much?"

"Sorry, Rachel." Danny pushed back the visor of his black helmet and ran a grimy hand over his face. "It's a long ride back from Brisbane, and I didn't want to be late and miss out on Mikey's birthday lunch." He grinned at the birthday boy, who'd wobbled to a halt. "Nice bike, mate. Happy birthday."

Fumbling in the pocket of his dirt-stained jeans, Danny pulled out a crumpled fifty dollar note. "I, uh, was pretty tied up with my parents in Brisbane, so couldn't buy you a present. Buy something with this next time you're in town."

"Ooh, thanks, Danny." Fifty dollars was a fortune to Mikey.

To Rachel, too. She couldn't believe the young jackaroo's generosity. She didn't pay him *that* well. But maybe his wealthy parents had slipped him something.

Danny nodded to her father. "Good to see you again, Mr. Barrington." The two had met shortly after Danny had come to work here, when her father had flown in unannounced one day to plead with her yet again to come home; his phone calls had been getting him nowhere.

"You, too, young man." Her father's tone was benign. Danny's upper-class accent and polite manner, Rachel mused, would no doubt excuse such flaws as a grubby appearance or a noisy motorbike.

"Well, I'd better have a shower and change," Danny said. "I'm a mess. I, uh, hit a muddy puddle on the way back and fell off my bike."

Rachel was surprised to hear that any puddles had remained after that brief downpour in the night, with the earth so dry and dusty. But at least it explained his filthy state. And he badly needed a shave, she noticed. Maybe he'd had such a good night at his luxury five-star hotel that he'd slept in this morning and hadn't had time before he left for his long ride back from Brisbane.

She shook her head as the motorbike roared off in another cloud of dust. ''Come on, Rocky.'' She tugged the pony forward. ''Back on your bike, Mikey. Let's get this birthday party under way.''

Let's get the confrontation between my father and Zac out of the way, was what Rachel was really thinking. Would Zac take her side against her father, or would they both gang up on her?

Mercifully, her father's initial encounter with Zac was cut short. With Vince and Joanne having joined Zac at the makeshift bar by now to share a beer, her father barely had a chance to exchange greetings with Zac before a yell from Mikey plucked Zac away.

''Look, Uncle Zac, Grandpa gave me a two-wheeler bike! You have to teach me how to ride it wifout twainer wheels.''

As Zac stepped over to admire the new bike, Vince and Joanne followed, surprising Mikey with crudely wrapped parcels of their own. All her father could do was stand back and look on.

Rachel poured him a beer as he watched, knowing he'd prefer a Scotch, but whiskey was beyond her means these days. She held out a bowl of peanuts, but he shook his head.

She turned away with a shrug, moving closer to her son. With luck, her father would realize she wasn't going to change her mind about selling and would leave straight after lunch.

"Wow!" Mikey gave a whoop. "My own stock whip! Thanks, Vince!"

It was a small, handmade stock whip, painstakingly plaited and polished, just like an adult one.

"You made it yourself, Vince?" Rachel eyed it in awe. It must have taken hours to do.

"No problem," said Vince. "Joanne's made somethin' for you, too, Mikey."

The birthday boy gave another shriek as he ripped open Jo's present. She'd carved a wooden boomerang for him, painting it with Aboriginal serpents and symbols, in a whirl of earthy colors.

"Wow! A boomewang! Can you show me how to throw it, Jo?"

Both were gifts that would have taken time, thought and care, Rachel thought, a lump welling in her throat. If her head stockman and his wife were trying to drive her out, would they have spent so much time and painstaking effort making these gifts for her son?

"How about I give you a demo now, Mikey?" Joanne reached for the boomerang. "Over here, away from everyone."

At an enthusiastic "Yeah!" from Mikey, with the others ambling over to watch, Joanne drew back a slender brown arm, took aim, and hurled the boomerang into the air with all her might. It spun away, whirling high over the sheds before turning in a wide arc and spinning back to land at her feet.

Rachel saw her father wince. "You'll need to be careful," he growled. "Those things can be lethal."

"Not if they're used properly," Zac drawled, and winked at Rachel, making her throat well up again. Was Zac's wink a secret message that he was going to stand by her and refuse to bow and scrape to her powerful father?

She gave him a smile, her warmest yet, bringing a heart-stopping smile to his own lips, an answering warmth to his eyes. She felt her knees go weak, the usual heat flowing through her like warm honey. If only this togetherness would last. If only Zac would decide to stay in Australia with her and Mikey indefinitely. If only he would go on being the Zac Hammond she was beginning to know, rather than the uncaring, irresponsible drifter Adrian had sworn he was.

"Want me to light the barbecue?" Zac asked, the sexy smile still on his lips. For a crazy second, she imagined he was really asking, *Want me to light your fire?*

She flushed, blinking away her fanciful musings. "Thanks, Zac. Ah, here's Amy and Joshua. Amy's husband, Todd, won't be coming," she told him. "He's too busy to leave his Roma medical practice. Mikey, here's Josh!" she called out as Amy's four-wheel-drive swung into the yard. Having Amy and Josh here should also help keep her father at a safe distance.

Mikey gave a squawk and ran to meet them, Rachel close behind. After she'd welcomed them and introduced them around, she watched as Mikey opened yet another present to reveal a large, yellow toy truck. As he squealed in delight, she excused herself. "I'll start bringing the food out onto the veranda."

Joanne heard her and swung round. "I'll come and help you."

"So will I," said Amy, taking a quick sip of the drink Zac had handed her.

"You've only just arrived, Amy," Rachel said, pausing. "You stay out here and finish your drink." *And keep my father amused.*

But Amy insisted. "I'll bring my drink with me," she said. "Besides, I've something to tell you." Her gentle eyes glowed, and Rachel smiled and nodded, hoping that her friend's longtime attempt to have a second child was the reason for her radiance.

"I'll bring the meat out for the barbecue." The offer came from Vince. "Hope it's still fresh, with the power failure an' all."

"Power failure?" Her father's dark-browed gaze pinned his daughter before she could swing away. "Your power is off? You've no refrigeration, no electric fans? In this heat?"

She waved a dismissive hand. "Someone'll be here to fix it soon. Why don't you take your drink up onto the veranda, Dad, in the shade, if the heat's bothering you?"

"It isn't. I'll stay here and watch over my grandson," he muttered, giving her no choice but to leave him alone with Zac and the two boys. She knew her father wouldn't let it lie there, not the tenacious Hedley Barrington. He'd grill Zac—and Danny and Vince, too, when he had the chance—until he'd heard it all. Not just about the power line being cut, but about the water bore being wrecked and the fence wires being cut, with maybe even a mention of the shot kangaroo. She cursed silently.

By the time she and her two helpers had carried the salads out to the birthday table on the veranda, with Mikey's monster cake an impressive centerpiece beneath the brightly-colored balloons, luscious aromas and clouds of smoke were rising from the sizzling steaks, chops, homemade sausages and beef rissoles on the barbecue below.

Vince tended the barbecue while her father, young Josh and a clean, freshly shaven Danny stood around watching Zac teach Mikey how to ride his two-wheeler—without the training wheels.

Her father did not look happy about it. He was watching his grandson like a hawk, his huge frame tensed, as if ready to rush to the rescue if Mikey looked in danger of coming a cropper. But Zac was watching the boy just as carefully, making sure nothing untoward happened to him.

She knew that nothing would. She could trust her son with Zac. She'd sensed it before and she was sure of it now. Zac, while encouraging Mikey's independence, was also encouraging him to be safe, to be careful, to become proficient at each challenging new skill, despite his tender age. And Mikey was just as determined to learn and triumph.

"The meat's ready!" Vince shouted. "Come and get it!"

Zac somehow managed to pluck Mikey away from his new bike as everyone converged on the barbecue, grabbing plates and choosing the meat they wanted.

They drifted from there to the shady veranda to help themselves to salads and crusty bread, either standing to eat or finding a place to sit.

Rachel buzzed back and forth, making sure the two boys and Amy had enough to eat and drink. She was determined to keep busy, anything to avoid a direct confrontation with her father, who'd been trying to catch her attention from the moment she'd summoned everyone to lunch.

His face was grim, and she knew he must have heard by now about the damage to the property—if not from Zac, from Vince and Joanne. He'd probably heard about all her other problems too—the lack of feed and water, the weakened cattle and maybe even the bank's withdrawal of help. Few people managed to keep secrets in the outback.

The last thing she wanted to listen to was her father sounding off about her many failures and the gruesome dangers and other problems she'd be facing if she stayed here.

But she knew she was just putting off the inevitable. Her father wouldn't leave until he'd had his say. He was determined to crush her resistance to selling Yarrah Downs, and he'd use her responsibility as a mother and the vulnerability of her son—his grandson—to get through to her.

But what could he do, when it all boiled down? He couldn't *force* her to sell and leave. She just had to stay strong. With luck, Zac would back her up and convince her father that she would have him here to help her, and that he was here for the long haul.

But *was* he? Would Zac make such a commitment? She still wasn't sure that he would.

Chapter Seven

"Can we light the candles now, Mummy?" Having waited as patiently as a jiggling four-year-old could for everyone to finish eating, Mikey was eager to blow out the candles on top of his monster cake.

"Yes, darling. Come and stand over here. Gather round, everyone!" Rachel lit a match and set the four candles alight. As Mikey leaned forward to blow them out, they all sang "Happy Birthday."

Zac produced a camera and started clicking away— the kind of thoughtful gesture, Rachel reflected, that was becoming typical of him, making her wonder how her husband could have been so wrong about his brother. Had Zac changed over the years? Or had Adrian simply closed his mind to his brother's good points?

After Mikey had blown out his candles to claps and cheers, Rachel helped her son thrust a knife into the cake and told him to make a wish. He blurted out his wish without a second's hesitation. "I wish Uncle Zac would stay here forever and ever!"

There was a momentary pause before everyone cheered again—everyone but her father, Rachel noticed. As for her, she gave a careless laugh and avoided Zac's eye as she took the knife from Mikey and began slicing the cake into large pieces, one for each guest. If Zac was showing any discomfort or wariness, she didn't want to see it.

As she was handing round the birthday cake, Mikey announced in his loudest, highest voice, "Mummy killed a big snake today. It was by our back door. I nearly trod on it."

She winced. Oh, her father would love hearing that!

"A snake?" She felt rather than saw her father's large frame tense in his chair. "Snakes come into your yard to threaten my grandson?"

"Mummy killed it with a spade," Mikey said with relish. "Wam! Wam!" He chopped the air. "It was a mulga snake. They're *deadly*."

Rachel refused to look at her father. She glanced at Zac, instead, half expecting to see disapproval in his eyes for killing the native wildlife. But she caught a gleam of something else. Surprise? Approval? Certainly not the horror her father would be showing.

"No big deal." She shrugged and raised her chin. "As Mikey said, I dealt with it. That's what you do in the bush—you deal with things. You have to be prepared for anything.'' *Even having to say goodbye to the man you long to be with.* ''I'll get the coffee.''

She escaped to the kitchen, cursing the fact that the power was still off. Without a fan to cool the kitchen, she soon felt beads of sweat break out on her already flushed face as the wood stove heated up. If that electric-repair truck didn't show soon, everything remaining in the fridge and freezer, and in the cool room out in the shed, would be ruined.

''Can I lend a hand?''

She gulped in a quick breath before turning around, relieved that it wasn't her father, yet not so sure it was a relief to see Zac. Mikey's guileless wish that his uncle Zac would stay forever still spun in her ears.

''Uh…thanks, Zac. You could help me hand around the coffee in a sec.'' Afraid that he was about to name a specific departure date and shatter any illusion she might have that he intended to stay at Yarrah Downs indefinitely, she babbled on to cover a flutter of apprehension.

''Thanks for taking the photos of Mikey, Zac. I don't have any recent ones, and none by a professional photographer.'' Her own modest camera had long since run out of film. Film was a luxury she couldn't afford. ''I guess you'll want to take a few photos of Mikey with you…when you go.''

She snapped her mouth shut, wishing she'd shut it before that last bit came out. What the heck was she doing? *Forcing* him into naming a departure date? Letting him think she'd be prepared when the time came for him to go because she'd never expected him to stay?

Oh, Zac, I want you to stay here at Yarrah Downs forever, just as Mikey does!

Yet despite her disquiet, the need to know was too strong to resist. "You must be missing your *real* photography, Zac, missing your wild animals and those wild, remote places. What *are* your favorite animals, by the way?" *As if I care...*

His lips eased into a slow, dangerously attractive smile. "My favorite animals? I'm rather partial to Santa Gertrudis cattle right now, and stock horses, and cattle dogs...and a certain little black-and-white pony."

She felt a lump knot in her throat. Did he mean that, or was he just putting off naming a date because he didn't know how long it would take to track down that wretched vandal and get Yarrah Downs back on its feet?

Don't try to pin him down, you fool. Just enjoy him while you have him. She didn't even want to think about how she would feel when he did leave, how Mikey would feel.

Amy burst into the kitchen with a stack of plates. "Rachel, that was a lovely lunch!"

Rachel blew out the breath she hadn't realized she was holding. "Thanks, Amy. Coffee coming up," she said brightly, turning back to the stove. If Amy had sensed any tension in the room, she'd shown no sign of it. Being happily pregnant, as she'd confirmed before lunch, she'd no doubt have only one thing on her mind at the moment.

Rachel poured the coffee into a row of waiting cups, which Amy and Zac helped to carry out to the veranda. Everyone had stayed for coffee but the two boys, who'd raced off to the training paddock to see Mikey's new pony. Rachel stuck close to Amy, swapping confidences about babies and childbirth, effectively blocking out any approach by her father.

When Hedley Barrington eventually put down his empty cup with a clatter, she hoped he was making a move to leave. It was already late afternoon and she knew he'd want to fly out before dark. Added to that, he was an impatient man, a busy man, who hated wasting time.

And he must be feeling that today was a complete waste of time. She'd made it as difficult as she could for him, giving him no chance to take her aside and start laying down the law in his usual domineering fashion.

But her father made no move to leave just yet. He collared Zac, instead.

"I hope you're going to talk my daughter into giving up this drought-stricken, out-of-the-way place." He boomed out the words, seeming unconcerned who might be listening. Even from across the veranda she heard him clearly.

"A crumbling outback cattle station is no place for a young widow with a small child. Especially with a criminal on the loose and deadly snakes threatening my grandson. It's not a safe or suitable environment."

"I won't let anything happen to your daughter or your grandson, Mr. Barrington," came Zac's laconic reply.

Rachel's heart lifted. She still had Zac on her side. Glancing at her father, she saw he didn't like Zac's answer. Not one bit. His heavy brows were lowered in a way that she'd learned in the past was ominous.

"You're encouraging my daughter to stay on here, despite the danger she's in?" Hedley Barrington used the tone he'd used countless times before to subdue a recalcitrant business opponent. "I don't think you realize the true situation, Zac. Not only the danger my daughter and grandson are in right now, but the difficulties they face out here without a husband or a father. Now that Adrian's gone, this harsh outback life is not for them."

His deep voice vibrated with passion as he pressed home his point. "They belong back in Sydney with me. I can provide for them, give them protection and a better life, give them anything they want."

Rachel sprang from her chair. This had gone far enough. But her father didn't heed the warning as she advanced toward him. He was in full flight now, determined to have his say.

"I need my daughter back. She was trained to take my place at Barrington's, and I need to continue that training...now, before it's too late. I'm an old man with heart problems. I lost my wife last year. I need to know that Barrington's is going to be left in good hands."

Rachel rolled her eyes. So now he was appealing for sympathy, playing the ailing old man, the aging widower who didn't have much time left. Any man less frail she had yet to meet. He might be overweight, but this was the first she'd heard of any heart problems.

"My daughter tells me you're only here for a visit,

Zac, so I assume you haven't come back to buy the property yourself...or have you?'' Her father's sharp eyes turned cunning. ''With my help, Rachel could afford to let you have it for a song.''

She felt a choking sensation. Only her father would be so outrageously presumptuous, so crassly insensitive, so infuriatingly high-handed and assume that she would go along with him, meekly selling her property at a loss because she had a father rich enough to support her in the future.

Giving Zac no chance to reply—or perhaps fearing what his answer might be—she let her swelling anger erupt. She wasn't Hedley Barrington's daughter for nothing.

''It's time you left, Father. You're spoiling Mikey's birthday. I told you I don't intend to give up Yarrah Downs and I meant it. I won't be coming back to Sydney to live—ever. You'll have to find someone else to take over Barrington's. It's never going to be me!''

Even as she spoke, she wondered if she believed her own words. Was she really going to be able to stay on here, even with Zac's support, if the drought and her other difficulties continued?

Her father heaved himself around to face her, still making no move to rise from the wicker armchair he'd wedged himself into. ''If it's loyalty to your husband that's keeping you here, Rachel, I think there's something you should know.''

As she glared at him, wondering what on earth he was talking about, there was a scuffle from behind as Vince, anxious to avoid brewing trouble, pushed back his chair. "We'd better get back to work. I wanna go and check on that calf. Coming, Jo? Danny, the gate to the training yard's coming loose. Can you fix it?"

Joanne was quick to jump up. Danny moved more slowly, as if reluctant to miss a family dispute. A chorus of thank-yous floated back as they left.

Amy, looking uncomfortable at being caught in the crossfire, rose too. "Time I was heading back home myself. I'll grab Josh on the way. Thanks, Rachel, it's been great. Bye everyone." She turned and made a dive for the veranda steps.

"Want me to keep an eye on Mikey, Rachel, when his mate Josh goes?" Zac started to haul himself out of his wicker chair. "I could give him another pony ride. Or a bike ride."

"No!" Her sharp tone stopped him. "Danny will be there to keep an eye on him. I want you to stay, Zac." Whatever her father's diabolical mind had cooked up now, she might need a witness. Or at least some moral support.

She swiveled around to glower at her infuriating parent. "See what you've done, Father? You've ruined Mikey's party. Why can't you butt out of my life? There's nothing you can tell me that I could possibly want to hear."

"You prefer to close your mind to the truth about your husband?"

The truth? Her brow puckered. What on earth was he talking about? She knew she should have simply walked away, but the need to hear more immobilized her. Only Zac was within earshot now, and he should know if this so-called revelation about his brother was the truth or not.

She didn't trust her father. Not for a second. He would try anything to get her away from Yarrah Downs. She planted her hands on her hips and thrust out her jaw. Attack, she thought, had always been her father's chosen method, and she was his daughter, after all.

"You've never forgiven Adrian for rejecting your loathsome offer of money, have you, Father?" she almost spat at him. "Well, I've never forgiven you either, for doing something so despicable."

She spun around to explain to Zac. "My father tried to buy Adrian off when he heard we wanted to get married. He offered him a million dollars—a *million*, can you believe it?—to get out of my life. Adrian refused. He wanted me, not my father's filthy money. I was so outraged I refused to speak to my father again until after Mikey was born. I only gave in then because of my mother."

She'd kept in touch with her mother all along, but only by phone. Loyalty to her husband and wanting to present a united front had kept her mother at Hedley Barrington's side.

"You would have thanked me if Adrian had accepted my offer and promptly ditched you." Her father waved away a fly buzzing round his nose. "What your husband never told you—what *I've* never told you—was that he and I made a deal."

Her heart stopped. "What kind of a deal?" Adrian had told her about the huge bribe her father had offered him, but he'd never mentioned any subsequent deal.

Her father smirked. "Adrian told me he'd be happy for you to take over Barrington's when I needed to hand over the reins. He promised he would make sure you came back to Sydney when the time came. He said that by then any children you had would be away at school and you could work for Barrington's during the week and fly back to Yarrah Downs weekends."

"I don't believe you!" She felt herself shaking, as much with shock as anger. Adrian would never have made such an outrageous commitment without consulting her, without ever mentioning it. Would he?

Her eyes raked her father's face. Could it possibly be true? Adrian had never breathed a word about such a deal—one he must have known she would never agree to. On the other hand, she recalled how Adrian had often pressed her into patching things up with her father. He'd been the one who'd talked her around after Mikey was born, telling her how sad her parents must be not to know their grandson and persuading her to let them fly in to see him occasionally. He'd even put in a sealed airstrip suitable for her father's jet, waving aside her objections that they couldn't afford it.

He'd never told her exactly *how* he'd managed to pay for it, and his haphazard bookkeeping hadn't explained it. Now she wondered if her father had paid for it and other things as well. But it hardly mattered now...not after this latest bombshell.

She flicked her gaze to Zac. "Do *you* believe it?"

He shrugged his broad shoulders, his gray eyes impassive under his tumbled mop of dark hair. "Adrian's gone now, Rachel. Does it matter? He could have just made that promise to keep the lines of communication open, hoping for an eventual reconciliation between you and your father. Which was what happened, right?"

A reconciliation of sorts, Rachel mused dryly. But at least it had made her mother happy and had given Mikey the chance to know his grandparents. But it must also have given her father hope that she would ultimately change her mind about refusing to come back to Sydney and taking over Barrington's one day.

"Whatever deal you might have made with Adrian, Father," she said, still wondering how her husband could have gone behind her back and if she'd ever known him at all, "it wasn't anything to do with me. I knew nothing about it. So you might as well give up. It's never going to happen."

"The point is," her father said, tenacious as ever, "your own husband believed your future was with me. With Barrington's. He was going to actively encourage you to take over when I'm ready to retire. So your loyalty to him—and to this parched, remote back-of-beyond—is misplaced. Now that he's gone, you have no reason to stay on here. He never *expected* you to stay."

Rachel felt a wave of nausea. But only fleetingly. Adrian wasn't the reason she'd stayed here. She'd grown to love Yarrah Downs and the outback. Mikey loved it, too. She had no desire to go back to the city, and she certainly had no wish to take over Barrington's.

"But your daughter *wants* to stay here, Mr. Barrington," Zac quietly reminded him. "She won't be struggling alone, as you put it. I'll be here."

Her father shot daggers at Zac. "So I have you to thank for this obstinate stand my daughter persists in taking, have I? You've made her believe she'll always have your support. Very brotherly, I'm sure. But for how long will she have it? You're a professional wildlife photographer. You're not going to stay around here. Not in the long term."

Rachel held her breath, hardly daring to look at Zac, afraid of what she might see. Afraid of what she might *hear*. And worried he was going to admit to her father that his interest in her was more than brotherly and that Mikey was his son. But she'd begged Zac not to say anything until she'd told Mikey, and he'd given his word.

"I have no plans to leave." Zac's tone was steady, relaxed. Whether he meant it or not, she felt her tension easing, gratitude flowing through her. "I intend to help your daughter track down this lowlife who's been vandalizing the property and give her a helping hand getting the property back on its feet."

As Rachel's heart jumped in renewed hope, she thought her father was going to burst a blood vessel. The veins in his forehead were bulging in an alarming way.

"Didn't you hear what I just said about your brother?" he roared at Zac. "He never expected Rachel to stay here indefinitely. So why would you want to support her stubbornness? You ought to be encouraging her to sell, as her husband would have wanted her to do. If you want to keep Yarrah Downs in the Hammond family, with Vince to run it for you when you're not here, you can have it as a gift. Gratis. My daughter won't lose out.''

Rachel gasped. A *gift?* ''You have no *right,* Father!'' She turned on him in a fury, concerned he might be getting through to Zac. Was her brother-in-law at all tempted by her father's latest preposterous offer? Handing him Yarrah Downs on a plate, for heaven's sake!

''I've told you, I'm staying put,'' she repeated, ''whether Zac stays here or not. This is my home, and it's Mikey's home, and nothing's going to change that. Come on, Father, I'll see you back to your plane. It's time you were going.''

As she urged her father to his feet, Zac unfolded his long, lean-hipped frame and stood up. ''I'll be with Mikey,'' he said, and his eyes met hers for a brief second, which was all she needed. There was something in that warm, fleeting glance that gave her heart.

''Thank you, Zac.'' She gave him a smile, hoping she wasn't being naive. Her father's offer would surely tempt even the strongest of men. Adrian had believed that Barrington's would eventually lure her back to Sydney. Why wouldn't Zac believe it, too?

''Let's go, Father.'' She spoke coldly, implacably. ''It's getting late.''

She would allow her father to say goodbye to Mikey on the way, but she would stay close to make sure it was a brief farewell. She didn't want her father seducing Mikey with offers of a more exciting, more pampered life in the big city.

Zac's eyes grew speculative as he noted the protective way Rachel hovered over her son, holding on to the boy's narrow shoulders until her father stomped off toward the airstrip, his powerful frame hunched in angry frustration. She stayed close to Mikey until the Citation jet was a tiny speck in the sky.

"It's been a tough day for you," he commented as she visibly relaxed. Mikey immediately leaped away from her to snatch up his boomerang from the dry grass where he'd dropped it.

"Watch me throw it, Uncle Zac. Jo showed me how. But I'm not too good at it yet."

"Fire away." As he stood watching the boy's determined efforts, Zac glanced around to see Rachel looking at him, the warmth in her clear blue eyes dazzling him.

"Thank you for sticking up for me today, Zac. My father can be ruthlessly persuasive—as he tried to be with Adrian before I married him. I admired Adrian for standing up to my father then, for not being tempted by his despicable bribe, but I had no idea he'd promised my father he'd put pressure on me to go back to Barrington's."

Her shoulders slumped. "How could Adrian have done such a despicable thing behind my back? I feel I didn't know him at all."

Zac had some murderous thoughts himself, but what was the point in adding to her pain by blackening his brother's name any further? Let her keep what illusions she still had. Adrian was dead now, and the shabby deal between Barrington and his son-in-law would never be put to the test.

"Rachel, you have to put it behind you." He kept his tone dispassionate, hiding the deep anger he felt. "You only have your father's word that there was a deal in the first place. Adrian's not here to dispute it. Forget it and get on with your life."

"That's what I'm trying to do." Her eyes were bleak, making him long to take her in his arms and kiss away her torment. *Tonight. Maybe tonight.*

"Do you think we'll ever save Yarrah Downs, Zac?" she asked in a muffled voice. "Even with your help? You can't stop the drought. And how can you catch that slimy vandal when we have no idea who it is?"

"We'll find him, Rachel. I reckon we can discount Vince and Joanne. They both convinced me, separately, that they were camped out at the Ten Mile all night, sheltering in the shed up there from that downpour we had—around the same time that someone was cutting your power line, miles away."

She nodded, relief in her eyes. "I'd hate to think it was either of them."

"And Danny was in Brisbane last night with his parents—though we could always check on that, too."

"I can't imagine Danny having any reason to be involved in this. Why would he want to drive me out? He's only a kid, here for experience as a jackaroo."

Zac shrugged. Experience had taught him that people were like wild animals. They could be extremely cunning and unpredictable, and it wasn't always obvious what motivated them. It was wise to be continually on your guard.

"The sooner we get Bazza back here to keep an eye on you and Mikey during the day, the better," he growled, feeling frustrated and hogtied for the first time in his life. It would be a help if they knew who their enemy was and what they were up against. "With Bazza here, I won't have to worry about you and Mikey being left unguarded when I'm out and about."

"I can look after Mikey," she was quick to reassure him. "I'm not afraid, Zac."

He noted the way she straightened her shoulders and lifted her dimpled chin as she said it. Searching her eyes, he saw the same glint of determination he'd seen in Hedley Barrington's.

"No, you're the bravest woman I know," he said, letting his eyes caress hers. His arms ached to caress other parts of her, *every* part of her. "But a few precautions won't go amiss. In fact—" he checked his watch "—I could go and find Bazza now, while Danny's here in the yard fixing that gate. Capable as I know you are, I'd feel better knowing you're not here alone. Can I take your four-wheel-drive?"

"Sure. No problem."

"I'll try to be back with Bazza before dark." He lifted a hand to stroke her soft cheek, wishing more strongly than ever that he could stroke the rest of her and feel the smoothness of her naked skin under his fingers. *Soon,* he thought. *Very soon.* "You just enjoy what's left of our son's birthday."

He felt satisfaction when she didn't react to his saying *our* son. She accepted it. She believed it. Believed that together they'd brought Mikey into the world. Perhaps now she'd be willing to take the next step.

He felt a stirring in his loins, his body turning to a slow-burning fire at the thought.

Chapter Eight

Despite the sweltering heat in the house, Mikey fell asleep as soon as he crashed into bed, worn-out after his long, action-packed day.

Rachel was tired herself, emotionally drained after the heated battle with her father earlier and her uncertainty about the future. She dearly wanted a good night's sleep, but she wanted Zac more. However late he was coming home, with or without Bazza, she was going to wait up for him.

He'd stood by her today. He'd defied her father, resisted the bullying tycoon's outrageous bribes, his most forceful efforts to induce him to change sides.

Before he'd married her, Adrian had rejected an equally exorbitant bribe from her father, but *his* rejection had come with conditions. She needed to believe that her husband had only made that secret deal with her father to prevent a permanent split between father and daughter, hoping to pacify her father until both sides had cooled down.

If she didn't hang on to that belief her entire marriage would have been a sham, a marriage based on deceit and lies.

But whatever the truth behind her husband's reprehensible promise to her father, it was obvious to her now that Adrian and Zac, despite being identical twins, were indeed very different, yet not in the way Adrian had led her to expect.

Far from being the irresponsible, selfish, uncaring loner that her husband had insisted he was, Zac had shown, from the moment he'd come back to Yarrah Downs, that he was dependable, considerate and genuinely caring. And she'd come to believe that what she was seeing was the true Zac.

Hurry home, Zac. She crossed her arms and hugged them tightly to her body, imagining it was Zac holding her. For the first time she wanted to tell him she was glad he was here.

As dusk fell she began to light candles in the house, but they only made the rooms feel hotter. She wandered out onto the vine-covered veranda, still bedecked with balloons, and sank into a wicker armchair. Buster settled at her feet.

The clouds of last night had long cleared away and there wasn't a breath of wind, though the beginning of an autumn crispness had crept into the air, giving promise of some relief from the heat. But no relief from the drought.

She'd heard Vince and Joanne arrive back some time ago, their shouts echoing across the yard as they met up with Danny before retiring for the night. She wondered what they were all doing now. With no power at the homestead, there'd be no video-watching, no keeping cool under ceiling fans, no reading in a good light. They'd probably already gone to bed. Stockmen normally retired early, because they rose at dawn and worked such long, hard days.

She tensed in her chair as a man's voice drifted across the yard. Buster's tail thumped, as if it was someone he knew. "Who's there?" she called out, more out of curiosity than alarm. "Is that you, Vince?"

Danny emerged from the shadows, his fancy satellite phone clamped to his ear. "Okay…right…speak to you later."

He strolled up to the veranda. "Sorry, Rachel. Didn't mean to startle you. Just calling my mother to thank her for a great night. I get better reception out in the open." He clamped a hand to his head. "*Yeow!* A rotten headache's been giving me hell for days. Reckon I'll take a couple of aspirin and turn in."

"You poor thing, Danny. If it's no better in the morning, you'd better see Amy's husband, Todd— he's a doctor in Roma. You'll find his number on a board in the bungalow."

"Yeah, I might do that. Thanks."

She sighed as he disappeared into the trees around his bungalow. If he had to go to Roma tomorrow, it would mean another day off.

But she didn't want to think about Danny. She wanted to think about Zac.

She pressed her hands to her chest, wondering if he'd truly meant it when he'd assured her father he intended to stay on at Yarrah Downs. Or had he just said it to get the old tyrant off her back? She let a sigh out through her teeth. How *could* Zac stay, when his work—his exciting, adventurous, highly valued photographic work—took him all over the world?

The low growl of an engine brought her head up sharply, her heart picking up a beat. The sound grew louder, closer. Zac was back! She ran down to the yard to meet him. And Bazza, hopefully.

Before she reached the dust-covered vehicle, Zac had jumped out and opened the passenger door. "Rachel, come and meet my old friend Bazza, coming back home where he belongs."

A short, sinewy old man with wiry gray hair and a grizzled beard climbed out, ignoring Zac's helping hand. She darted forward, wanting him to know he was welcome.

"I'm so glad you've come back, Bazza. May I call you Bazza? I'm Rachel."

He shrugged, eyeing her warily. She was the widow of the man who'd sent him away. It was understandable he'd be wary.

She tried to reassure him. "I can only apologize for whatever happened in the past, Bazza. It was a terrible misunderstanding. This is your home, and nobody will make you leave it again." She realized she was accepting Zac's word over her husband's and hoped she was doing the right thing. In her heart she was sure she was. Zac's father had made a commitment to keep Bazza on at Yarrah Downs for life, and Zac intended to honor that commitment, as her husband had failed to do.

"I've prepared a room in the bungalow for you," she told him. "Our jackaroo, Danny, has one of the other rooms. You won't mind sharing the bathroom and kitchen?"

Bazza grunted. "You don't need to fuss over me, Mrs. Hammond."

"Rachel," she said again. "Nobody here calls me Mrs. Hammond."

"Bazza could bunk down anywhere and be happy." Zac touched the old man's shoulder in a gesture of affection. "Baz and I used to go out camping together, sleeping under the stars. Don't worry, Baz, it won't be too luxurious here. There's no power, as I warned you. You'll have no electric lights, no fans and no fridge, which'll mean roughing it until the power line's repaired."

Rachel wondered if Zac had told Bazza about the other attacks on Yarrah Downs and how they were hoping he'd lend a hand watching over the homestead. Was that how Zac had persuaded the old man to come back?

"I've put a battery-operated lantern in your room, Bazza," she told him, "and some extra food in the kitchen—mainly canned food." She grimaced as she glanced up at Zac. "They're taking their time coming to fix our power line."

"It's only been one day. Someone should be here by tomorrow. Come on, Bazza, I'll take you to your

room, introduce you to Danny if he's still awake, and
then you can get some shut-eye. You can meet the
others in the morning. Mikey will think you're Santa
Claus," he said with a chuckle, "when he sees that
beard."

Bazza grunted, but it was an amiable grunt this
time. He likes kids, Rachel thought, and felt some
relief at the thought. A lot of old people found small
children a nuisance, and Mikey could be noisy and
exhausting.

"We're so happy to have you back, Bazza," she
said. "See you in the morning." She would leave it
to Zac to settle in the old man. If Bazza didn't want
any fuss, that was fine with her.

But she hoped Zac wouldn't be long. Now that he
was back, she wanted him more than ever, her pulses
skittering at the thought of being alone with him very
soon now, her smoldering gaze seeking his in the
moon's pearly glow.

Zac caught the warm light in Rachel's eyes before
he swung away and hoped it meant what he'd long
dreamed and yearned for—guiltily during the years of
her marriage and more hopefully since he'd been
back. Especially now that they appeared to have put
their past mistakes and misunderstandings behind
them.

It was the same look he'd seen five years ago, after
they'd soared to the heights of rapture in each other's
arms, but the loving warmth in her eyes hadn't been
for him then. At least, not consciously. But he, Zac,
not her husband, had ignited that passion in her, and

that thought had kept a flicker of hope alive all these years.

Now it was different. She no longer had a husband in her life, and she was looking at him with those same warm eyes again, and this time she knew who he was.

Was he reading more in her tender gaze than was there? Could it simply be gratitude he was seeing for the support he'd given her today in standing up to her father, rather than the more intimate emotion he longed for?

There was only one way to find out.

He found her on the moonlit veranda, skimpily clad in a halter top and shorts, her golden hair a loose veil round her bare shoulders. She had coffee ready to pour and a smile that pulled his heartstrings tight. It pulled other parts of him tight as well. For a second he couldn't speak.

"The beer's not cold, so I thought you might welcome some coffee, instead." Her voice was slightly unsteady, which sent a rush of added heat through him. It had to be more than gratitude she was feeling. She was nervous, on edge, just as he was. Hope soared.

Now, he thought, blood pounding in his brain. *Make your move now, while you have her alone and in a responsive mood. Don't let this chance slip.*

He ignored the coffee she'd poured for him. "You waited up for me." His eyes caught and held hers, his gut wrenching as the moonlight washed over her face. God, she was beautiful. "You've had a long day. You must be worn-out." *What was he doing? Putting the idea of sleep into her head?*

"Not anymore." She took a step closer, her wide blue eyes steady on his, her breasts thrusting against her brief top. An owl hooted in the trees, and Buster's head came up sharply.

Tempted as he was, Zac didn't touch her. Not yet. But his body was aching with almost unbearable tension.

"Zac, I'm glad you're here. I'm glad you came back. And I'm glad you've brought Bazza home." She reached up and held her soft palm to his face, the light touch exquisite torture. He wanted to grab her hand and press it to his lips, but she hadn't finished and he wanted to hear what she had to say first.

"You're a good man, Zac. I…I know it now. I've realized it for some time. I can't understand anyone thinking otherwise." *Adrian,* she meant. Adrian, who must have maligned and derided him throughout their short-lived marriage. Had she finally stopped believing his brother's lies and slurs and grown to trust the uncaring, irresponsible twin brother?

"That means a lot to me, Rachel."

She slid a hand around his neck, a sexy invitation in her eyes, her fingers warm on his skin. He felt her soft breasts brushing his chest, her heartbeat quickening under his, and heat flared through him. Sweet heaven, she was seducing him again, just as she had five years ago, only knowingly this time, wanting *him,* not Adrian. He waited, his body coiled tight.

She raised her face to his, her delicate fragrance seeping into his nostrils, her lips full and inviting, drawing his hot gaze like an irresistible magnet. "Let's put the past behind us, Zac, once and for all."

He felt his throat constrict, his heart lift. She was letting him know she'd forgiven him for what happened five years ago, that she no longer believed her husband's lies and innuendoes. They could start fresh and move on. Her body was telling him even more.

He couldn't wait a second longer. With slow deliberation, rather than the frenzied, unrestrained hunger of five years ago, he gathered her in his arms, bent his head and covered her mouth with his. Her lips softened and parted, sweet, moist and warm under his.

His long-repressed need for her threatened to overwhelm him. But much as he ached to take her the way he had before, with hot, mindless passion and searing, uncontrolled lust, he curbed the powerful urge, wanting it to be different this time, wanting to show her he could be tender and patient, as well as wildly passionate, wanting to taste and savor this sweet moment he'd waited so long for.

He moved his mouth leisurely over hers, letting her drown, slowly and thoroughly, in a series of deep, drugging kisses.

Rachel thought she might faint under the heady sensations spiraling through her. Her limbs felt as if they were dissolving into warm, flowing treacle.

There was no impatience in Zac this time, no blazing loss of control. He seemed intent on giving her pleasure, on savoring the taste of her lips while slowly, deliberately kissing her senseless, tantalizing her with the exquisite promise of what was to come.

And they had all the time in the world—if she survived his melting, mind-numbing kisses.

When they finally surfaced for air, gulping in deep, gasping breaths, Zac clamped one arm round her waist, slid the other under her knees and swept her up into his powerful arms—something no man had ever done to her before, though she'd dreamed of it often enough over the years, and only ever with Zac as her fantasy hero.

She'd always awoken from her dreams feeling guilty and frustrated, with a fierce, helpless yearning inside her, but now, this time, she was already wide-awake, in the arms of the man she'd dreamed about for so long, a man who was tangible flesh and blood. And there was no need for guilt or frustration because she was a free woman now, with nothing to stop her, nothing to stop him, no obstacle in their way.

She moaned in delicious expectation.

Buster's earsplitting barks rent the air, a jarring intrusion.

"Quiet, Buster," she pleaded as the muscled arms holding her stiffened. But the pesky blue heeler didn't stop. She opened her eyes and saw Zac's face. He was frowning, his head raised and alert, his nostrils flaring, sniffing the air.

"Do you smell smoke?"

Oh, no! She moaned silently. *Not a bushfire. Not now.* She sniffed tentatively, a coldness creeping into her languid body as she smelled it, too.

"It's close!" she whispered. "Where is it?" Her feet hit the floorboards with a thud as Zac withdrew his arm from under her knees. Her legs, still weak from his kisses, almost buckled beneath her as she tried to stand.

But Zac had no intention of letting her fall, his other arm still gripping her waist firmly as they both lurched to the edge of the veranda and peered out into the moonlit gloom.

There was no evil glow visible, no glimpse of flames or smoke, but any relief was short-lived. Someone came running from the direction of the bungalow across the yard, followed by a more shadowy figure.

''The machinery shed's on fire!'' It was old Bazza, scurrying across the yard like a man thirty years younger, clutching what looked like a blanket. Behind him was Danny, stumbling as he ran, as if he'd been woken from a deep sleep.

Zac grabbed Rachel's hand and leaped down the veranda steps, then charged around the side of the house. Now they could see it, too—flames leaping from the open front of the machinery shed. The galvanized iron walls were still standing, but something inside the shed was alight.

Rachel's throat clenched. The tractor, the plough, their precious tools! *Oh dear God!*

Bazza was already beating at the flames when they reached the shed, with Danny grabbing the fire extinguisher on an outer wall and directing the foam at a pile of spare tires. Bazza was trying to save the tractor alongside, the fire having reached one of its huge tires.

Rachel screamed for Vince and Joanne as she and Zac grabbed whatever they could find and joined in the fight to save the shed and its contents. Between them they managed to douse the flames and bring the fire under control. Mercifully, thanks to Bazza's quick action and keen sense of smell, they'd caught the fire in time. No serious damage had been done.

Burrowing around for the source of the fire, Zac shouted, "Looks like it started here, with these spare tires. And this could be the cause." He pointed to a drum of diesel oil nearby. After examining it more closely, he straightened with a frown. "The drum's been punctured. There's a small hole near the base. The oil must have seeped out gradually and spread across the floor."

He took a step sideways and bent low over the pile of burned tires. He glanced up with a curse. "There's the remains of what looks like a candle down here. The seeping oil must have reached it and caught fire, setting the tires on fire."

He cast an accusing look around. "Who the hell left a lighted candle in here?" No one spoke up. "Well, someone must have." A chorus of denials followed.

"It doesn't have to be one of us." Danny's tone was indignant. "Whoever cut your power line and wrecked your bore could have crept in here after we'd all gone to bed."

"Yeah. It must be that damned intruder again." Vince seized on the suggestion. Too quickly? Rachel wondered. "All I know is, it wasn't Joanne or me." He shot a look at Bazza, as if he wasn't so sure about this outsider who'd been thrust on them. A man who could be bearing a grudge, Vince's narrowed eyes seemed to suggest.

"Want me to grab my bike and take a look around?" Danny asked. "He might still be on foot, making for a car or a horse he's left somewhere. I might be able to catch— *Yeoow!*" He clapped a hand to his head. "This darned headache! The tablets must've worn off. I was fast asleep when Bazza woke me."

"You go back to bed, Danny," Rachel said at once. "Whoever did this is probably long gone by now."

"I'll grab Maverick and check around." Zac touched her shoulder, a brief pressure of his fingers. "Vince, you and Jo take a closer look around the yards. Make sure everything's safe and secure. Rachel, you stay in the house with Mikey. I think you should go to bed—you've had quite enough to deal with for one day."

Rachel nodded, her chest lifting and falling in a sigh. He was telling her not to wait up for him, not to expect a resumption of their intimacy. The moment had passed, the mood had been shattered. But the gleam in his eyes before he swung away told her he hadn't forgotten, that there'd be another time, another chance.

She bunched her hands into fists. Why did this *fiend,* this sneaky, vindictive *lowlife,* have to keep on spoiling everything, threatening her home and her livelihood? And who in heaven's name could it be?

Chapter Nine

Rachel was preparing breakfast the next morning after retrieving what she could from her sad-looking vegetable garden when Zac came in from the yards. The smile he gave her made her heart skip sideways. There was a tinge of regret there, too, as if he was remembering last night. But as he gulped down his toast and coffee, his expression changed to steely resolve.

"We have to stop this son of a—" He glanced at Mikey. "This worthless good-for-nothing. He's gone too far this time. If that fire had spread…"

Rachel shivered. If it had spread to the house, with Mikey fast asleep in his bed…

She lifted her chin, refusing to be intimidated. "That wasn't likely, with everyone at home, ready to rush into the yard at the first hint of smoke. If he'd meant any personal harm, he would have set fire to the house, not the shed. I...I think it's someone who just wants to scare me into selling, not someone wanting to hurt any of us.''

''Yeah, but he's not succeeding, is he? You're not going to sell.'' Zac's tone was grim, but his eyes...

She gulped, catching a spark of admiration in the gray depths, and tenderness and concern. Not for himself, but for her. For her and Mikey.

''It could make him desperate,'' Zac growled, ''and spur him into doing something more drastic.''

''You found no clues last night?'' she asked without much hope. ''No sign of an intruder?''

''Not a thing. No strange tracks, no disturbed cattle, nothing. Vince found nothing suspicious back here in the yards, either. Unless *he's* the...'' He paused. ''Hey, Mikey, how about fetching your new stock whip? I know just the person who'll teach you how to crack it like a pro.''

''You mean you, Uncle Zac?''

''No, not me, mate. An old friend of mine who's come back here to live with us. His name's Bazza and he looks like Santa Claus.''

''Yeah?'' Mikey's eyes widened. ''Okay, I'll get it!'' He dived for the kitchen door, making his usual clatter as he scuttled off down the passage.

Rachel turned back to Zac with a worried frown. ''You're beginning to suspect Vince, after all?''

''Not really, but he was here last night, so who knows? I've sent him and Joanne out to fence off a boggy water hole I noticed from the air yesterday, up near Michael's Gap. We don't want any cattle getting stuck in the mud.''

''No,'' she agreed, cursing the drought that was adding to her woes. ''They're getting weaker by the day.''

Rising from the table, Zac put his hands on her shoulders. The comfort and warmth of his curled palms flowed into her, lifting her flagging spirits.

''The new bores will help when they're up and running.'' His deep, mellow voice was as soothing as his touch. ''I'll take the plane out again to check the cattle and make sure nothing looks amiss from the air. I can keep an eye on Vince and Joanne at the same time, and the guys putting in the new bore. I might be gone awhile.''

''Thanks, Zac.'' She managed a smile. Did he realize how much his presence, his moral support, meant to her?

His eyes burned into hers for a nerve-tingling second. ''I'll get Bazza to keep an eye on Mikey while I'm away and you're busy with your chores.'' His grasp on her shoulders tightened. ''Stay close to the house.''

''I intend to.'' She lifted her chin again, determined not to show the worry she felt. ''I need to catch up on some cleaning and washing. With the washing machine still out of use, I'll have to wash everything by hand. You be careful, Zac...'' She slid her hand over his, having visions of her daredevil brother-in-law flying dangerously low over treetops and wires to get a closer view.

A shudder riffled through her. If anything happened to Zac…

He bent his head and brushed her lips with his, a tantalizing, featherlike touch that left her quivering, wanting more. "You be careful, too. Danny won't be around for long, by the way." Zac's eyes seemed regretful as he raised his head. "He has a doctor's appointment in Roma later this morning."

"I'm glad he's getting his headache checked out," she said, hoping it was nothing serious.

"And I'm glad Bazza's here." Zac gave her shoulders a last reassuring squeeze, making her wish he'd stay a bit longer and squeeze other parts of her that were crying out for him. "You can rely on the old fella, Rachel. I'd trust him with my life."

"I like him, too, Zac. He's seems down-to-earth and genuine, and I can tell he likes kids. We'll be fine. Don't you worry. You just take care yourself."

Zac's tanned face creased in the most heart-melting smile she'd seen so far, a smile that flooded her veins with delicious waves of warmth. "I have an incentive now not to take any crazy risks," he said, holding her gaze again for a long, meaningful moment. "At least, I'm hoping I have."

"You have, Zac," she said, her eyes misting. And this time she was the one who kissed him, letting her lips linger on his in a tender, heartfelt pledge.

Mikey burst back into the room with his stock whip and pulled up, blinking. Rather than being fazed at seeing his mother kissing his uncle Zac in broad daylight, something he'd rarely witnessed with his mother and the man he'd known as his father, his rosy mouth widened in a broad grin.

"Are you and Uncle Zac gonna get married, Mummy?"

Rachel took a startled step back, her cheeks suffused with bright color. Would Zàc take fright at the word *married* and start backing off? Was marriage what she'd been secretly hoping for?

Adrian's words sprang back to taunt her. *My brother's not the settling-down type. He'll never care enough about anyone to want to settle down. He only cares about himself and his precious wildlife. No woman will ever change that.*

She gulped hard. *Oh, Zac, is that true?*

Looking down at her son rather than at Zac, she said briskly, "I was just kissing Uncle Zac goodbye, Mikey. He has to go out for a while." She almost pushed them both out the kitchen door. "It's time I did some work. I've a thousand things to do. Go with Zac, Mikey. He'll take you to Bazza." She didn't even glance at Zac as father and son disappeared into the yards.

Not long after that, she heard Zac's Cessna take off.

Midway through the morning, Rachel was hanging out some clothes, after laboriously washing them by hand, when she heard Buster barking—though not, thankfully, with the urgency of last night. It couldn't be the crack of Mikey's stock whip that was stirring him up, because that had stopped some time ago.

She wandered across the yard to check and found

Buster tethered to a post, straining at the rope and yapping in protest. Danny was sitting on his motor-bike nearby, his satellite phone to his ear.

"Oh, you're still here, Danny."

He abruptly cut off his call, whipped his free hand to his head and winced. "Just telling my mum about this damned headache. I'll have to leave for the doctor soon. Uh…Bazza and Mikey have started a game of hide-and-seek. See?" He pointed across the yard. "That's why Buster's tied up. He was spoiling their game. I, uh, didn't feel up to joining in."

"Poor Danny, I hope Todd can give you some re-lief. If it's a migraine, you might just need some stronger tablets. Have you had migraines before?"

"Nothing like this." Danny tossed her a mortified look. "Sorry I'm being so useless, Rachel. I'm real sorry." He actually sounded as if he meant it, which surprised her, because she hadn't thought of Danny as the type to apologize for anything.

"You can't help having a headache, Danny," she said, trying to coax a smile from him. But he must have been in too much pain.

"Bazza's real good with your kid," he mumbled, as if wanting to say something positive. "He's watch-ing him like a hawk. Means you can do your book-keeping or whatever you need to do and not worry about him."

Well, he *was* surprising her this morning. Danny wasn't usually so considerate. He must really be in pain! Or believed he had a serious disease.

"It *is* good having someone around to help keep an eye on Mikey," she admitted. "I do have a lot to catch up on. I need to clean the house before I do anything else. You just get yourself better, Danny.'' She gave him a rallying smile and caught a wobbly smile in return as she turned back to the house.

After mopping all the rooms with tiled floors, cursing the fact that she couldn't vacuum the carpets until the power came back on, she started flicking a duster around. There was a fine layer of dust on everything.

As she dusted the furniture in Zac's room, wanting to do something for him for once, she caught sight of his travel bags piled in a corner, noting that the one he used for his clothes was filthy. She could scrub it clean for him, or at least make it look a bit more respectable.

The bag looked empty, but she checked inside to make sure. She found a narrow pocket on one side. When she slipped her hand in, she felt some paper. Pulling it out, she saw it was an old, flattened letter. Some handwritten lines, in her late husband's familiar scrawl, jumped out at her.

I'm about to marry the Barrington Department Store heiress—aren't you jealous, twin brother? I'll have a fortune to spend on Yarrah Downs when she comes into her inheritance...

Rigid with shock, she sank onto the edge of the bed. Adrian was writing about *her,* gloating to his brother that he was about to marry, not a girl he was madly in love with, but an heiress who was going to provide him with a fortune!

Her hands were shaking, but she forced herself to read on.

The sweet irony is, Rachel's father, Hedley Barrington, offered me a million dollars—a cool million!—to get out of his daughter's life. He wanted her to marry a stuck-up city twit and take over the Barrington empire one day, not get hitched to an outback roughneck like me. I threw his offer back in his face. I'll get far more by marrying her, because she'll inherit the lot when her father dies. I'll be able to buy up other properties and turn Yarrah Downs into the best privately owned cattle station in Queensland...

Rachel felt bitter bile stinging her throat. *I'll get far more by marrying her...* Adrian had been a grasping, coldhearted gold digger, after all! He'd never cared about her, only about his beloved cattle station. She'd simply been the means to an end. Painful as it was, she kept on reading.

I've made sure Barrington won't cut off his daughter's inheritance when I marry her by making him a promise—that I'll talk Rachel into going back to Sydney and taking over Barrington's when he's ready to retire, or turns up his toes. I'll put up with having a wife who's not around all the time as long as I have Yarrah Downs and a bucket load of money to pour into the property...

Adrian was admitting he'd made that outrageous promise to her father! He was openly boasting about it, and worse, admitting he'd made the deal, not simply to pacify her father, but to make sure he didn't cut off his daughter's inheritance!

Oh, Adrian! She'd hoped, foolishly and naively, that he'd only made that unconscionable deal with her father to reconcile her disapproving parent to their marriage and prevent a permanent rift between father and daughter.

Now she knew better. Adrian had seen the glittering prize at the end. No wonder he'd tried so hard to reunite her with her father. And he'd succeeded in the end. Mikey's arrival *had* brought them closer, at least close enough for her to allow her father to come and visit his grandson occasionally.

She felt sick as she read on.

If Rachel refuses to honor my promise when the time comes, too bad. Her father will be pushing up daisies or too ill and weak to kick up a fuss. By then I hope we'll have given him grandkids to soften him up, and disinheritance will be the last thing on his mind…

Rachel gave a contemptuous shake of her head. Adrian had even been prepared to make use of his own children! And he hadn't been ashamed to admit his grubby plans to his estranged brother. He'd obviously trusted Zac not to come back and expose him. Was that a point in Zac's favor—or against him?

The whine of a motorbike drifted into her consciousness, but she was only dimly aware of it. The words on the page compelled her to keep reading.

Don't get me wrong—Rachel's gorgeous, the most beautiful girl I've ever met. I fell in love with her before I even knew who she was. I only found out she was an heiress after I proposed and she took me to meet her parents—the day her father tried to bribe me to keep out of her life—so don't go thinking the money's all I care about...

Rachel gave a snort. Was it a consolation, she wondered, that Adrian had proposed to her before learning who she was? Or that he'd thought her the most beautiful girl he'd ever met?

With a dead weight in her stomach, she read to the bitter end.

Eat your heart out, twin brother! I'm going to have it all one day—a beautiful wife and a fortune to spend on Yarrah Downs, sooner, hopefully, rather than later. Her father must be close to seventy. I feel sorry for you, Zac. What do you have to show for your life? Nothing! Still, no hard feelings. I'm writing to invite you to our wedding next week, though I'll understand if you can't make it in time.
Cheers, Adrian.

Rachel glanced at the date at the top of the letter and noted that it was written, not the week before their wedding, but the day before—too late to reach Zac in time or to give his brother a chance to get home. It was painfully clear that Adrian hadn't wanted Zac there, even though he'd told her he'd invited his brother in plenty of time and that Zac had ignored the invitation.

She felt her lip curling. It was obvious Adrian hadn't wanted to risk his twin brother warning his bride-to-be of his treacherous motives before he had his ring safely on her finger! Maybe he'd also been afraid that his precious heiress would prefer his twin brother to *him.*

She shut her eyes, disgusted and disillusioned at this latest evidence that her husband was not the man she'd believed him to be. And worse, she now had proof that Zac had known, from the day they first met five years ago, that she was an heiress to a fortune.

Did Zac share his brother's mercenary nature and covet her father's millions, too? Was that the real reason he'd come back? Hoping for a share of the booty? He *was* Adrian's identical twin, after all.

Had Zac coveted his brother's wife, as well, that night he'd turned up on her doorstep five years ago while her husband was away? Had Adrian's self-satisfied taunts been niggling at Zac, finally spurring him into retaliating, irresistibly challenging him to win the ''beautiful heiress'' away from his brother?

Had Zac been jealous of Adrian's good fortune?

She groaned aloud, staring at the letter in her hand, only half-aware of the sound of a plane coming in to land, amidst another barking frenzy from Buster, tied up outside. All she could concentrate on in her current devastated state was the poison she'd just read and how it must have affected Zac.

He must have forgotten he still had the letter. She'd only found it because she'd delved deep into that narrow side pocket. He'd be horrified to know that she'd found and read it. If he'd wanted her to know the truth about her gold-digging husband, surely he would already have told her.

But whether he'd kept quiet to shield her from the harsh facts about the man she'd married or to protect himself, because he had similar covetous designs on her fortune…

She slipped the letter back into the side pocket of Zac's soiled travel bag and dumped the bag where she'd found it, no longer having the heart to clean it, let alone hang on to the letter. Adrian was no longer around to face him with his sins, and Zac…

She blinked away a sting of tears. *Oh, Zac, can I trust you?*

She thought she'd come to know him since he'd been back. He'd struck her as a caring, honorable man, a self-sufficient, big-hearted man in control of his own destiny. He'd never struck her as the scheming, mercenary type.

She filled her lungs with air and released it in a long, tremulous sigh. How *could* she know what Zac was really like, what he was really thinking or wanting? She hadn't known her own husband!

As her newfound happiness and trust came tumbling down around her, she became aware that somebody outside was shouting her name. And Buster was going crazy, incensed at still being chained up.

It hit her then for the first time. That plane she'd heard... Zac must be back!

She gulped in another mouthful of air. She hadn't expected him back so soon, wasn't sure she *wanted* him back so soon. How would she be able to face him after Adrian's soul-destroying revelations—revelations she'd barely had time to absorb?

And why the heck was old Bazza yelling like that? Above his shouts and Buster's frenzied howls, she heard the roar of a plane. Zac was leaving again already?

What in heaven's name was going on?

With a pounding heart, she ran from Zac's room and out onto the veranda.

Bazza, wheezing and out of breath, came stumbling up to the steps. "Mikey's gone!" He pointed shakily behind him. "The man in that plane snatched him and took off. It all happened real quick!"

Her blood froze. *Oh, my God, it wasn't Zac.* Looking up, she saw a glint of silver high in the sky, fast disappearing to the south. Toward Sydney. Not a Cessna, but a corporate jet. A familiar Citation jet!

"My father!" It came out in a disbelieving croak. Her father had snatched Mikey! She stamped her foot in frustration. Why hadn't she realized it was her father's plane from the different sound? Her face stung with guilt. *Because Adrian's mind-numbing letter and my nagging doubts about Zac blocked out everything else!*

"That white-haired man was your father? Mikey's grandfather?" Hope gleamed for a second in Bazza's crinkled black eyes, but died a quick death under Rachel's fury and obvious alarm. "You didn't know he was comin'?"

"No, I didn't know. Oh, Bazza, I never thought my father would go this far, never for a minute. He…he's kidnapped Mikey!" It was a despairing wail.

Bazza's weathered face screwed up in agonized self-reproach. Zac had relied on him to keep the boy safe. "It's all my fault."

"Oh, Bazza, you mustn't blame yourself." Pulling herself together, she patted the old man's bony shoulder, anger at her father overriding her despair. "Blame my father. And me. I should have known it was his jet and rushed out the second I heard it. Buster, stop that din!" She leaped down the steps to release the straining blue heeler, who at once shot off through the trees in the direction of the airstrip.

"If Buster hadn't been tied up," Bazza growled, his grizzled head downcast, "this mightn't have happened."

She tried to reassure him. "I doubt if Buster would have gone for my father. He was only here yesterday, for Mikey's birthday." *Bearing gifts. Ingratiating himself with my son.* What, she wondered bleakly, was he promising Mikey right now? The flashy, beguiling wonders of the big city?

A shiver ran down her spine. "Tell me exactly what happened, Bazza. Did my father say anything? Did Mikey?"

"They never even saw me. I wasn't close enough." He blew out a wheezy sigh. "Mikey and I were playin' hide-'n-seek. He wasn't meant to go outta the yard. I'd count to fifty an' he'd run and hide. But that last time he made me count to two hundred, 'cause his legs were small, 'e said, an' he couldn't run far.''

Rachel felt tears sting her eyes. How like Mikey, she thought, to come up with a crafty excuse like that, so he could run farther, hide farther away, in the time allowed.

''Go on,'' she urged, hiding her growing fears. Her father would never have attempted anything this drastic without a well-thought-out plan and the confidence he'd come out on top. *Oh, Zac, where are you? I need you. Mikey needs you.*

She heaved a shuddering sigh. Adrian's letter to Zac didn't matter. Only Mikey mattered.

Bazza shuffled his feet in the dust. ''I heard the plane comin' in while I was searchin' for Mikey behind the sheds. I ran to the airstrip to check it out, callin' out to Mikey on the way. I saw this fancy jet on the tarmac an' a white-haired man climbin' out. But I was still a fair way off.''

He hauled in another wheezy breath. ''Then I saw Mikey run outta the fuel shed where he'd been hidin' and the old man picked him up and bundled him into the plane. It was gone before I got close enough to do anythin'.''

''Danny is already gone, I take it?'' she asked, remembering that the jackaroo had still been around while the two were playing hide-and-seek.

''Yeah. He'd left just before. Anyway, he'd've been no help. He was too crook.'' His beard drooped to his chest again. ''I wasn't no help, neither. Your husband was right, I'm past it. I can't be relied on. Zac's gonna to want me gone, too.''

''No, Bazza!'' She couldn't bear to hear the torment in the old man's voice. ''At least we know where Mikey is. My father would never hurt him.'' But to get his own way he'd hurt *her*.

''Listen!'' Her head jerked up at a new sound from above. It was the familiar drone of a light plane, coming in from the north. ''Zac's back!'' she cried, relief flooding through her. Zac would know what to do. He would know how to get Mikey back, without giving in to whatever ruthless demands her father might have in mind. If only he'd come back sooner!

She started running. Bazza hobbled after her.

Chapter Ten

Zac landed the Cessna smoothly on Yarrah Downs's sealed airstrip. He'd covered every inch of the property, diving into gullies and flying low over trees, and seen nothing amiss. Vince and Jo were still fencing off the boggy water hole and the contractors he'd hired were where they were meant to be, sinking a new bore. The cattle looked undisturbed.

On his way back, he'd spied an electric-repair truck below and a man inspecting the cut power line. About time!

As he cut the Cessna's engine, Zac saw Rachel running across the dry grass to meet him, her hair escaped from its neat braid and flowing behind her in a gleam of sunlit gold.

His gut lurched in longing. Now *this* was the kind

of welcome home he could get used to. Maybe, if they could persuade Bazza to mind Mikey for another hour or so...

He jumped down from the plane, ready to snatch Rachel into his arms and make some smart crack about her missing him. But one look at her face, her stricken eyes, and the roguish gleam faded from his eyes. Something was wrong. Seriously wrong.

He grasped her tanned arms and felt her trembling. "Rachel, what is it? Is it Mikey?" There was no sign of him. There was only old Bazza, hobbling behind her through the dry grass, and Mikey's blue heeler sniffing about near the fuel shed. "Where's Mikey?" His voice sharpened. "Has he been hurt?"

He felt a razor-sharp pain such as he'd never felt before. With everything that had been happening lately...

He closed his hands over Rachel's trembling shoulders. She needed his strength, needed positive vibes from him, not weakness or doubts. "What's happened?"

"Oh, Zac!" Her voice broke on a sob. "My father's snatched Mikey! He flew in while Mikey and Bazza were playing hide-and-seek. He just grabbed him and flew straight out again. I...I was still in the house." Her eyes were dark blue pools of pain. "Don't blame Bazza," she begged. "He feels bad enough already. Blame *me*. I left them alone too long!"

Her anguish sliced through him. If he'd had his hands on Hedley Barrington's neck at that moment... He felt her wince and realized he was digging his fingers into her skin. He loosened his grip and massaged her shoulders gently.

"The only one to blame, Rachel, is your father. You can't watch an active little kid every second."

He raised his hand and stroked her cheek, trying with the power of his gaze to wipe away her pain and fear. "We'll get him back, Rachel. You're his mother. Your father has no rights and he must know it." Was that a comfort? She didn't look very comforted.

He felt a wave of frustration that he couldn't fold her in his arms and kiss her, love her, the way he wanted to. The way he'd been wanting to for five long years. The way he'd almost managed to do last night. Almost...

"You don't know my father." She compressed her lips, but they were still trembling. "He'll have some diabolical plan. He always does."

She straightened, her blue eyes hardening. "Well, he's not getting away with it. I'm calling the police! Come on, Zac, let's get back to the house." She hooked her arm through his and started dragging him away.

Bazza, huffing and wheezing, lumbered up to them, a bowed, woebegone figure. "I ain't to be trusted, Zac. You better take me back to my hut. Won't do no harm there."

"You're not going anywhere, Bazza. We need you here." Zac reached out to briefly grip his old friend's bony arm. "I don't want to hear any more talk of blame from either of you, understand? We have to *think*. Put our heads together and think about what we need to do to get Mikey back. Danny's already gone to Roma, I take it?''

''Yes, not that long ago.'' Rachel tugged at his arm. ''Come on, Zac.''

As they tramped off through the scorched grass, he said to her, ''You know, it's funny—''

''Funny?'' She looked aghast.

''Not that kind of funny. I mean, it's funny your father should choose just the right moment to swoop in—while I was out in the Cessna, you were inside the house, Mikey was down by the fuel shed hiding from Bazza and the others were safely away, too.''

''What are you getting at, Zac? Are you saying…my father must have known our movements in advance? That he had inside information?''

''It could have happened quite innocently. Even you might have inadvertently given something away. Did your father call you this morning, making out he was concerned for your safety and asking what we were all doing?''

''No, he didn't.'' She chewed on her lip, then frowned. ''But I guess he could have seen Danny with his satellite phone yesterday and called *him*. It'd be easy enough to get hold of a phone number and to call from his jet. I did see Danny speaking on his phone before he left, but he said it was his mother. He'd have told me if my father had called…surely?''

''Maybe he didn't want to worry you.'' Zac jerked a shoulder, reaching down absently to pat Buster, who'd bounded after them. His mind was working overtime, but he kept his racing thoughts from Rachel. No point voicing vague suspicions without any real basis for them. But it might be worth doing some investigating of his own.

His chance came sooner than expected. The phone shrilled from the house, a bell on the veranda amplifying the sound. Rachel gave a choked cry and broke into a run. "That could be my father! Maybe he's had second thoughts and is bringing Mikey back."

Zac couldn't imagine Hedley Barrington ever having second thoughts about anything he did, but he nodded and waved her on. "You run. I want to check something with Bazza." Much as he wanted to go with her, he wanted to do something else first, before Danny came back from the doctor.

"Bazza…" He turned to the old man, who eyed him uneasily.

"I'm real sorry, Zac, for lettin' Mikey outta my sight. I should never—"

Zac cut him off midsentence. "Take me to your bungalow, Bazza. I want to have a look around."

"Sure, Zac. I got nothin' to hide. Search around all you want. What are you lookin' for? I ain't got no fancy cell phone, if that's what—"

"It's not *your* room I'm interested in, Bazza. It's Danny's."

The old man's bushy eyebrows waggled. "Rachel won't like that. Danny says she never comes into our rooms. She says it's our own private space, long as we're here."

"Just take me there, Bazza, before Danny comes back." *And before Rachel gets off the phone and insists on Danny's right to privacy.* "You can stand watch."

"Anythin' you say, Zac."

* * *

Rachel snatched up the jangling phone. "Yes?"

"Ah, Rachel, my dear—"

She gripped the receiver. "Have you gone mad, Father? Where's Mikey? What have you done with him? What are you—"

"Calm down, Rachel. Mikey is fine. He's here in the plane with me, having the time of his life." He dropped his voice. "You've driven me to this, Rachel. I've been worried sick about my grandson. About you, too. I had to do something drastic to make you see sense."

"*Sense?* You think what you're doing is *sense?* Kidnapping my son!"

"I didn't kidnap him, Rachel, I *rescued* him. My grandson isn't safe with you in that remote, drought-ridden backwater. I've proved that by finding him wandering down by the fuel shed among the tinder-dry grass and the snakes. No one was watching him. I could have been anybody. A criminal. A vandal. Even a *real* kidnapper. That'll weigh heavily against you, my dear, when I sue for custody."

"Custody! Are you crazy? You wouldn't dare!"

"You've forced me to resort to these lengths, Rachel. I'd do anything to ensure my grandson's safety and well-being—and yours, too, only you don't seem to care what happens to you. Don't you realize how vulnerable my grandson is, stuck out in that remote station with you—a struggling widow, living alone in the outback in intolerable conditions, with a vandal on the loose?"

Rachel felt herself trembling. Her father was so powerful, so devilishly clever, so obscenely rich. *Could* he take Mikey from her? Or was he just bluffing?

Damm it, she was a Barrington too! She could stand up to him. She *had* to.

"You think you can blackmail me into coming back to Sydney, Father, by snatching Mikey? I'm his *mother.* Your threats don't scare me."

No? She could feel her father's suffocating net tightening around her, dragging her inexorably away from the free, independent outback life she'd made for herself, the life she'd grown to love. He knew she would do anything for Mikey, give up anything in the world to hold on to him, even if it meant…

A deep shudder shook through her.

"I'm not trying to scare you, Rachel. It's my grandson's safety I'm thinking of, and he's safe and sound with me. He certainly had no security with *you*. *You're* not safe out there, either."

"You don't care about our safety!" She winced at the shaky tremor in her voice. "You only care about Barrington's and having me back in the family business. You think holding this threat over me will bring me back to Sydney? Well, think again!"

Call his bluff. Yes, that was what she had to do. Convince him he wasn't going to win, that she was never going to cave in. Even though in her deepest heart…

"It's not a threat, Rachel, it's a promise. With the money and resources at my disposal and the top legal team in the country ready to expose your precarious, totally inadequate living conditions and the very real danger you're in, I'd have no trouble winning custody.''

He let that sink in for a moment before adding coolly, ''But you do have a choice, Rachel. If you agree to sell and come back where you belong, I won't resort to the courts. I won't need to.''

She squeezed her eyes shut. She mustn't listen. ''Where are you taking Mikey? To your home?''

''*Our* home,'' her father corrected. ''It's your home, too, Rachel.''

''Oh, Father, that was a long time ago. I've been married and widowed since then. I have a new life now.''

''A life that's crumbling beneath you. I'll buy you a brand-new home when you come back, and I'll enroll Mikey at the very best schools. You and my grandson will have everything you could possibly want.''

Everything but our freedom, our happiness, our independence. Rachel felt a vicelike pressure in her head and chest, as if the room, the whole world, was crushing in on her, crushing out hope. *Zac, why aren't you here? Where are you? What are you doing? I need you!*

No! She clenched her jaw. This was *her* fight, hers alone. She'd put enough of her problems onto Zac's shoulders. She had to stand on her own two feet. She wouldn't have Zac here forever. She'd always known that.

''I'm calling the police!'' She spat out the threat.

"What you've done, Father, is criminal. Kidnapping is a crime."

"You think you'll be able to talk the police into taking on Hedley Barrington?" her father scoffed. He sounded infuriatingly calm and confident. "I'd just tell them what I told you—that I'm looking after my grandson for his own safety and well-being and that the courts will decide what's best for him."

She made a strangled sound in her throat, but he hadn't finished. "It's not as if I'm hiding your son away, Rachel. I've made no secret of what I've done or where I'm taking him. I'm simply making sure he's safe and properly cared for—in a secure home. Which is more than you can provide."

She panicked, hope sliding into desperation. "I...I'll get a court order!" Was that what she'd need? Broke as she was, she'd find a way to pay for it somehow. "Then you'll *have* to hand Mikey back."

"I won't hand him over quietly, Rachel. I'll call in the media and tell them you're putting my grandson's life in jeopardy. Is that what you want? Glaring publicity? The whole world knowing you're Hedley Barrington's daughter? Knowing that you and your son are living alone in the bush, at the mercy of intruders, vandals and maybe even *real* kidnappers, who could demand a huge ransom because Mikey is my grandson? Who do you think you'd have to turn to *then?*"

The room spun. She might have fallen if a powerful arm hadn't snaked around her waist to support her, drawing her into a strong, sheltering, familiar cocoon of warmth. Zac! She'd had no idea he was there or when he'd slipped into the house, hadn't been aware of anything but her father's head-spinning threats.

"Think about it, Rachel." Relentlessly, her father pressed home his point. "You can't stay at Yarrah Downs. Dangers aside, you're not even making ends meet. The place is a disaster. It's time you realized it and came back to Sydney. Agree to do that and to work with me at Barrington's until I hand the reins over to you, and you have my promise I won't sue for custody of my grandson."

He paused, then said, "I'll refrain from speaking to my lawyers until I have your answer, Rachel. Don't worry about Mikey. He's happy as a lark. I'll call you again when we reach Sydney."

As the phone clicked in her ear, she sagged against Zac's chest. She was shaking so badly she couldn't speak.

He pressed his lips to her tangled hair. "I'll get him back for you, Rachel," he vowed, steel in his voice. "If an old guy like your father can snatch Mikey from under our noses, I can snatch him back. Just tell me where your father lives."

"Oh, Zac." Despite herself, her lip quivered. How typical of him to want to rush to the rescue against all odds! But that was Zac. He'd never sit around helplessly, just waiting, hoping her father would come to his senses and back down. He would do something, take action, no matter how dangerous or how futile.

"My father's house is a *fortress,* Zac. High fences, security alarms, guard dogs, armed bodyguards. If I know him, he'll have already hired a nanny to keep a close watch over Mikey every second. Poor baby. I know what it's like. That's how *I* was brought up. I was still fighting for my freedom in my teens.''

Zac pulled her closer, wrapping her in his warmth. ''I'll find a way. You'd be amazed, the impenetrable fortresses I've overcome through the years to get close enough to wild animals to photograph them without being spotted. I'd have made a good cat burglar if I'd wanted a life of crime.''

She blinked away a helpless tear and shook her head, feeling her love for him expand almost to bursting point. ''Even if you managed to get in, Zac, and succeeded in getting Mikey out, it wouldn't solve anything, not for long. My father's threatening to sue for custody if I don't agree to come back to Sydney. Back to Barrington's.''

At Zac's scornful snort, she jerked back. ''Don't dismiss it as a bluff, Zac. He's serious. And he's rich enough and powerful enough to win—if I let it come to court.''

''You're not thinking of giving in, are you?'' Zac stared at her in disbelief. ''You'd actually go back to Sydney to work for your father rather than take him on in a custody battle? You're Mikey's mother. A loving, caring *mother*. No one would ever take him away from you.''

''Oh, Zac, it's not just the court battle, he's thought of everything. He *would* win, I'm telling you.'' She let the rest pour out, all the arguments and threats her father had thrown at her. When she paused at last, feeling helpless and wrung-out, she looked up at Zac with clouded eyes. She'd expected some words of comfort and support, or a show of defiance to give her some hope, but he'd barely turned a hair.

Moreover, he was looking downright smug. How could he take her father's threats so lightly when she and Mikey were in such a dire predicament?

She stepped back, breaking free of him, as her heart slowly constricted. Was Zac thinking that since her father held all the cards, they might as well give in, after all? That since *he* wouldn't be here at Yarrah Downs forever to help her look after Mikey, she'd be safer, better off, bowing to her father's demands and going back to Sydney?

Her hand went to her throat. Did Zac see this as his chance to get hold of Yarrah Downs for himself, even if he only planned to visit the place from time to time? Was he about to make her an offer? An offer couched in soothing assurances that he would continue the good work she'd begun here and come to Sydney to see her whenever he could?

Suddenly the stifling heat in the house seemed to engulf her, despair washing over her like a giant wave. What hope did she have if even Zac failed to support her?

"Rachel, don't look at me like that!" He reached out to her, only to drop his hand as she recoiled and took another step back. "We *can* win. We're the ones who hold all the aces, not your father."

She frowned, eyeing him uncertainly. What was he talking about?

"Your father's threatening to sue for custody of his grandson because he thinks you and Mikey are not safe here, right?" Zac eyes pinned hers. "He's worried stiff about this unknown vandal who's been making attacks on Yarrah Downs, fearing that you or his grandson might be next.''

''That's right,'' she said, searching Zac's eyes, bewildered by the confident, almost excited gleam in the silver-gray depths.

''Well, if we catch the vandal,'' Zac said, ''we'd get rid of your father's greatest concern. You'd no longer be in danger. He'd hardly be able to convince a court you're not safe at Yarrah Downs if we've removed the threat hanging over you.''

''And how do you intend to catch the vandal?''

''I think I know who it is.'' He actually smirked. ''I've found…some evidence.''

Her eyes flicked wide. ''What have you found, Zac? Who do you suspect? Tell me!''

''I think it's Danny,'' Zac said. ''I found a pair of insulated gloves and cutters under his…in his possession. The kind of protection he'd need to cut an electric power line. And a pair of spiked boots for climbing wooden poles.''

''That's crazy! Danny? It *can't* be Danny. He was in Brisbane with his parents the night that power line was cut!''

''A great alibi—if it's true. We only have his word for it.''

''We could check it out. Call all the hotels. Call his parents.''

''Hotel guest lists are confidential. And if Danny's as clever as I think he is, he'd have asked his parents to cover for him that night, spinning some tale about meeting a girl in Brisbane or applying for another job and wanting to keep it from you. They'd be dutiful parents and say he was with them.''

''But if Danny is the vandal, it means... Oh, Zac, it's impossible! He couldn't have lit that fire in the shed. He was asleep in bed with a terrible headache last night, zonked out with painkillers. He's at the doctor right now.''

''You can pretend to have a terrible headache. You can even fool a doctor. Think of the other things that have happened. The wrecked bore. The damaged fence, which *Danny* supposedly found. And the shot kangaroo dumped in the dam. He had the opportunity to do all those things.''

''But why? Why would Danny want to drive me out? He comes from a respectable, well-off family in Sydney, had a first-rate education and came with glowing references. He'd be mad to risk his reputation, his future.''

With a shrug Zac stepped over to the window, effectively breaking eye contact. ''Maybe it's just a boyish lark to him, an exciting challenge—who knows? When you're young, impetuous and cocksure, you take risks and don't think you'll ever get caught. He should be back here soon. Let me deal with it.''

''What if he doesn't intend to *come* back? What if he's finally got cold feet and decided to quit before it's too late and he's caught?''

''Oh, he'll be back,'' Zac said with grim certainty. ''All his possessions are still here.'' She wondered at the iron hardness in his voice. Was he expecting a fight? Expecting Danny to deny everything?

Or was he thinking of *her?* Her future, and

Mikey's, too, could depend on Danny's exposure as the vandal. She gulped hard, thinking of what was at stake. *Oh, Mikey, darling, we'll have you back soon, I promise. We'll get you back—Zac and I.*

She trembled, thinking of her father, so arrogantly sure of himself, so sure he'd covered every possible angle. *Would* he give up if they exposed Danny as the vandal?

Her stomach clenched. ''Even if it is Danny,'' she said, a bleakness creeping into her voice, ''my father will never give up. He'll still say we're not safe here, that there are other dangers, or that I'll go broke, or that the drought will ruin me and drive me out in the end. It's not just the vandal he's worried about.''

Zac swung back to face her. His grim expression had given way to quite a different look, a tenderness that pierced her heart. ''Danny's not our only trump card,'' he said gently. ''We do have another. We must tell your father the truth, Rachel. That Mikey is my son.''

A hopeful spark lit her eyes for a fleeting second, then died. Panic gripped her. ''No, Zac! W-we can't. We mustn't!''

His eyebrows shot up. Underneath, his gray eyes looked almost wounded. ''Would it hurt now that Adrian's gone? You *are* sure he's my son, aren't you?''

''Yes, Zac, of course I'm sure!'' She caught his arm. ''Adrian was meant to come home from his trip down south the night after we...after you left Yarrah Downs, but he ended up in hospital with acute appendicitis. Then he caught an infection, which kept him in hospital even longer. He was really weak when he came home, too weak to…'' She trailed off, knowing it wasn't necessary to spell it out.

Her eyes clung to his. ''*You're* Mikey's father all right, Zac. But if we tell my father what happened that night, he…he'll twist it around and turn it into something dirty. I know him. He'll accuse me of being promiscuous and disloyal to my husband, and you of being reckless and irresponsible—not fit parents to bring up his grandson. And he'll make sure it all comes out in public! I…I couldn't do that to Mikey.''

''I won't let that happen, Rachel. There'll be no publicity and no court case. I'll make sure of that.'' He sounded so confident. But then, Zac always did. *Rely on me,* he'd said to her once. But *could* she? Dared she? How could he be so sure?

He impaled her with a gaze of pure molten silver, as if trying to inject his self-assurance into her. ''Just don't weaken, Rachel. I know you're worried about Mikey, but you mustn't let your father bully you into doing what *he* wants. When he calls again, stand firm. Make no promises. I just need a bit of time.''

Zac didn't explain and she didn't need to ask. He needed time to tackle Danny. ''Where's Bazza?'' she asked suddenly, knowing how badly the old man felt about what had happened, and hating the thought of him being alone right now, torturing himself with guilt and self-recrimination.

''Bazza?'' The intensity in Zac's face eased. ''He's in your kitchen, making coffee and finding us something to eat.''

''He is?'' Dear Bazza. She should have known he

would want to do something helpful, not just brood about on his own. "I'd better go and help him. With this heat and no fans, I haven't even baked any fresh bread. And the cold meat's probably already starting to go bad—" Her head came up sharply. "Listen!" She glanced up. The ceiling fan above had started whirring. It was already stirring the hot, cloying air. "The power's back on!" She would have clapped her hands if she hadn't been so worried about Mikey.

As she raised her face to the welcome draft of air, she heard another sound—the noisy whine of a motorbike. Danny was back!

Zac touched her arm. "You stay with Bazza. Have some coffee—you must need it. And stay close to the phone. I'll report back."

"Zac, be careful," she begged. Danny was young and strong, and if cornered...

Assuming he *was* the vandal. "We could be wrong," she warned Zac. "He might have a perfectly logical explanation for having those gloves and cutters. Don't do anything rash!"

Zac's mouth curved in a wry grin, though the glint in his eye held little mirth. "No, boss. I'll be the height of restraint."

Zac Hammond, the height of restraint? She could almost hear the ghostly echo of his twin brother's derisive laughter.

Chapter Eleven

Zac ambled up to Danny as he dismounted his motorbike.

"Well, Danny, are you going to live?"

The young jackaroo gave a weak grin. "The doc put it down to a bad migraine and gave me some pills. Its not as bad as it was." He flicked a glance around. "Where is everybody?"

As if you don't know… Zac smiled grimly. "Danny, I want to show you something. Come with me." He waved a mystified Danny into the communal bungalow. When they reached the door of Danny's room, Zac said casually, "In here."

Danny balked. "In *my* room?" Now his eyes did show something—alarm?—but he covered it quickly

with anger. "Our rooms are meant to be private! I
bet Rachel didn't—"

"Just step into your room, Danny, will you?"
Zac's voice had turned to steel. He followed Danny
in and stood blocking the doorway. "I found something interesting under your bed—a pair of insulated
gloves and cutters. And a pair of spiked boots. Been
cutting any power lines lately?"

"No!" Danny's tanned face reddened in outrage.
"Someone must've planted them there. It's obvious!"

"I think not. I'm having them checked for finger-
prints," Zac drawled, bluffing without a second
thought. "If yours are found on them, you'll have
some explaining to do."

Danny paled, even under his tan. He glanced toward the door.

"You're not thinking of making a run for it, are
you?" Zac threw out the challenge with a cold half
smile, laced with scorn. "No, you wouldn't leave
without the money."

"Money? What money?" Danny shot a panicked
look in the direction of the bed.

"Go on. Take a look," Zac invited. "It's still there
where you hid it—under the mattress. Thousands of
dollars in cash." He took a gamble. "Someone's been
paying you a lot of money to do their dirty work for
them, haven't they, Danny? To wreck bores and light
fires and cut power lines—"

"No!" It was an enraged squawk. "It wasn't me!
I was in Brisbane when that power line was cut. I was
in bed with a rotten headache when that fire started.
I was at the doctor when…" He stopped, realizing

too late that he wasn't supposed to know what had happened today in his absence.

"When Hedley Barrington snatched Mikey?" Zac finished helpfully. *Got him,* he thought. "Look, Danny, let's not mess about. We know you've been working for Barrington, trying to force his daughter into selling. You've tried every means, short of physical violence, to demoralize Rachel and drive her out. Even planting deadly snakes."

"No! I had nothing to do with the snake, honest, Zac! I never did anything that could hurt them!" Danny looked quite sick, and Zac saw stark fear in his eyes. "Okay, I did the other things. But I wasn't working for Mr. Barrington. I did it for my…my uncle. He paid me to do it!"

Good try, Danny. Zac's mouth twisted. Barrington must have put the fear of death into the kid, extracting a promise not to implicate him if the young jackaroo got caught.

But at least Danny was admitting he was the vandal. That was a start.

"Now why would your uncle pay you big money to become a vandal?" he asked with a sardonic smile.

The answer came so quickly that he knew Danny must have already planned to use it if necessary. "My uncle wanted to buy an outback cattle station. When he heard that the owner of Yarrah Downs could be selling, he suggested I, uh, try to hurry things along. Without actually hurting anybody."

"So I just need to find this uncle of yours…"

"Won't do you any good. I've got five uncles, all farmers, and they'll all deny knowing anything about it.'' Danny's jaw jutted out, but Zac caught a flare of apprehension in his eyes. ''I never meant any harm to Rachel,'' he wailed. ''I just wanted her to do what everyone else wanted her to do—sell and go back to Sydney. It's what her own father wants.''

''And you, Danny, are in the best position to know what her father wants,'' Zac said evenly. His eyes stabbed the young jackaroo's. ''Don't insult my intelligence by spinning fairy tales about an uncle, Danny. I know Hedley Barrington paid you to vandalize the place. You've already given yourself away. You *know* he's snatched Mikey. You're the one who let him know when it was the right time to fly in!''

Another bluff, but who else could it have been? Danny was on the scene until just before Barrington flew in to grab Mikey. Their satellite phones would have made communication easy.

''I didn't!'' Danny bleated. ''I wasn't even here!''

''You were here until shortly before Barrington flew in.'' Zac's eyes flayed him. ''*You* suggested the game of hide-and-seek. *You* suggested tying up Mikey's dog.'' Bazza had told him that earlier. ''And *you* suggested Mikey hide in the fuel shed and make Bazza count to two hundred before going looking for him.'' Another guess, but there wasn't the faintest doubt in his voice—or in his mind.

Before Danny's white lips could form another denial, Zac clapped a hand on his shoulder and said in a more conciliatory tone, ''I know Barrington talked you into doing what you did, Danny.'' *Or the tycoon's money did.* ''You shouldn't have to go to jail while *he* gets off scot-free.''

"Jail!" Danny recoiled, his face taut with horror, his swagger quite gone. "You wouldn't call the cops! Zac, please! I'm not a criminal. I'm not dangerous. I never hurt anyone..."

Zac silenced him with a look that would have stopped a lunging tiger in its tracks. "You hurt *Rachel*. You damaged her property. You cost her a lot of money. And you scared her to death." He was glad his fearless love wasn't there to hear *that!* "Give me one good reason why I shouldn't hand you over to the police."

"I'll do anything you want, Zac. I'll tell you anything you want to know, if you'll just let me go! I'll even give all...all that cash to Rachel to make up for what I did. For what he made me do."

"He?"

"Mr. Barrington." Danny's shoulders slumped.

Yes! Zac smiled to himself.

Now that Danny had named Hedley Barrington, the floodgates opened. "He said he'd destroy me if I ever brought his name into it. That's why I've been so careful with alibis and covering my tracks. I didn't want to get caught. And it's why I said an uncle had put me up to it."

He stamped his feet in despair. "Mr. Barrington *will* destroy me if I try to put the blame on him. I *can't* dob him in, Zac. Not publicly. He's too rich and powerful—he can do anything. He could even destroy my family. He's threatened to. I...I'd rather risk jail than point a finger at Hedley Barrington!"

"It doesn't have to come to that, Danny, if you do

as I say.'' Zac reached behind him to pull the door shut. ''Now…here's what I want you to do.''

Rachel was doing her best to comfort a dejected Bazza, assuring him that her father was solely to blame for what had happened and that Mikey was fine and they'd have him home soon. But in her heart she wasn't so sure they would. Her father's ruthless threats had shaken her. He'd go to any lengths to have his daughter and grandson back in Sydney.

And if he succeeded in winning custody of Mikey—she stifled a groan—it *would* drive her back. She'd have no choice. She couldn't live without her precious son. If she wanted to be with Mikey, she'd have to sell and move back to Sydney.

She might as well give in now. She'd probably be forced into selling, anyway, before much longer, with this crushing drought and the bank's demands. Even if Zac did expose Danny as the vandal, her problems weren't going to go away.

She bit down on her lip in alarm. Why was Zac taking so long? If Danny was in the clear, Zac should have been back by now. She pressed a hand to her chest. *What are they doing?*

''Bazza, I'm going out to—'' She stopped. ''What's *that*?'' It was very clear what it was. The roar of a motorbike. And it wasn't coming toward the homestead, it was speeding away.

Oh, no, Danny's getting away! She ran for the door. Where was Zac? Had Danny flattened him before making a run for it?

''Something's happened to Zac!'' she yelled, rushing out of the house into the oppressively hot, sun-drenched yard. She could hear Bazza clumping un-evenly in her wake and feel Buster's furred warmth bumping into her legs as she ran.

Zac emerged from the trees outside Danny's bun-galow. She saw that he was rubbing his jaw. "Took me by surprise, the little brat!"

Danny had taken *Zac* by surprise? That didn't sound like the Zac she knew. She ran anxious eyes over him, but he seemed otherwise in one piece, as strong and muscular and sexy as always. She reached up and touched his rough jaw with tender fingers.

"Did Danny confess?" she whispered, though the jackaroo's hasty retreat, throwing a punch before bolt-ing was as good as a confession.

"Admitted everything. That's what caught me off guard." Zac's hand came up to cover hers as it lin-gered on his jaw. "He swore he was sorry, swore he'd already decided to stop what he'd been—"

"Shouldn't we go after him?" She seized his arm. Danny could be miles away already. "We could look for him in your plane."

Zac gave a dismissive shrug. "He won't be a threat anymore."

She stared at him. Devil-may-care Zac, always so quick to rush into action, to put boldness before cau-tion, wanted to let a confessed vandal go free? Danny must have hit him harder than she'd thought.

"How do you know he won't be a threat?"

"Because he doesn't *need* to make any more at-tacks on you, now that his uncle's found another property."

"His uncle?" She looked at Zac in confusion. "What are you talking about? What's Danny's uncle got to do with it?"

Zac tugged her into the dappled shade of a peppercorn tree, jerking his head at Bazza to join them. "Danny says his uncle put him up to all this. Apparently he's been looking for an outback cattle station. When he heard that your family were urging you to sell Yarrah Downs and move back to Sydney, he paid Danny to do what he could to hurry things along. Paid him so much he couldn't refuse."

"Lucky Danny." Her lip twisted in a sneer. "We should get the police onto both of them!" It made her angry that she had to think about Danny and his uncle, when all she wanted to think about was Mikey and her own desperate plight.

"Forget it." Zac lifted one shoulder. "We have no real proof. His uncle, whoever he is, swore he'd deny everything if Danny was ever caught."

"So Danny gets away with his rotten uncle's tainted money."

"Ah…not quite." Zac's mouth curved in a breath-catching smile, his tanned face crinkling in a way that almost made her forget about Mikey for a second. "Danny felt so bad about what he'd done to you, Rachel, especially when he heard about Mikey, that he wanted to give you the money his, uh, uncle had paid him, to help make things up to you. That's when he caught me unawares with that punch and took off."

Rachel looked at him dazedly, then bit her lip.

"And you believe him? You think he'll actually send us some of his…his ill-gotten gains?''

Some hope, she thought. More likely he'd just said it to put Zac off guard. Danny was an extremely clever, devious, conniving… "What did you mean by 'not quite'?'' She stared at Zac, puzzled.

"I meant, you already have it. The money. It's in this pouch." Zac pulled it from his shirt, where he'd stuffed it. "Danny might have already spent a bit, but there's still thousands here.''

"Thousands?'' She gaped at the bulging pouch.

"Yep. In cash." He thrust it into her hands. "Some consolation, I guess. Might help a bit. Shows that Danny's not all bad.''

"No.'' Gulping, she gazed up at Zac with misty eyes. If she knew Zac, he would have had a lot to do with Danny's sudden generosity, as well as being the one who'd unmasked the cocky young jackaroo in the first place.

"No,'' she repeated. "He can't be all bad.'' She drew down her brows, the mist in her eyes turning icy. "But my father is,'' she said, remembering the bleak future lying in wait for her if her heartless parent carried out his custody threat. "Oh, Zac, what are we going to do about Mikey?''

"I'll fly down to Sydney to confront your father,'' Zac said at once, grim purpose carving his face into granite. "Having disposed of our vandal, it's given us a strong bargaining point.''

Her body tensed. *He* was going to confront her father? She had a flash of déjà vu as her late husband's image rose to taunt her. *He'd* met with her father once, too. She thought of Adrian's letter to Zac, gloating about his future wife's inheritance and how it was going to be his one day, and for a brief, black moment, she wondered if Zac was planning to make some kind of deal with her father, the way his twin brother had.

She could still feel the roughness of Zac's jaw under her fingertips, but her hand was no longer touching him. It was curled into a white-knuckled ball, hidden by her folded arms.

The black moment passed. *Oh, Zac, I'm sorry.* She mustn't equate Zac with his brother. They might have looked as alike as two peas in a pod, but she'd seen for herself how totally different they were in every other way.

"I'll come with you," she said, her tone firm, belying the tremor that quivered below. "Mikey will want me there, too." But would her father agree to see either of them without an official order demanding his grandson's return? How long would it take to organize one? Days? Zac was offering to confront her father now.

"That might not be such a good idea." Zac's voice was infinitely gentle. "Your father *wants* you back in Sydney. He'll try to keep you there, do anything to keep you there."

"He can try all he likes!" she cried, but her heart wavered. Sydney was her father's power base, where he had his influential friends, his hotshot lawyers. What did *she* have? Nothing. Nobody. Nobody but Zac.

"Besides—" Zac's eyes softened, as if he felt her

pain, understood her frustration "—your father's going to call you when he reaches Sydney, right? What if he finds you're not here? If he suspects you're on your way to Sydney, he might panic and move Mikey to a place where we can't find him."

A strangled cry rose in her throat, erupting as a harsh laugh. "My father never panics."

"No? You don't call kidnapping his grandson a sign of panic? If he's desperate enough to do that, he might be desperate enough to spirit Mikey away if he believes you're on your way to reclaim him. Let me go alone, Rachel, and act as your intermediary. Your father and I just might be able to settle this between us."

Settle this between us. Why did that make her think of her late husband again? Adrian, the man she'd trusted most in the world, settling the matter of her future inheritance…

But Zac wasn't Adrian!

"I better go check on Rocky," Bazza said gruffly, reminding them he was still there. "Come on, Buster!" He scuttled off with his lopsided gait, diplomatically leaving her alone with Zac. Buster scooted after him.

She turned back to Zac to examine his bronzed face with searching eyes and a yearning heart, feeling a rush of love at everything she saw—the dark slashes of his eyebrows, the black, curling lashes, the glinting warmth of his silver-gray eyes, the wickedly sensual mouth—yet still conscious of a tiny niggle of uncertainty.

"You think my father would listen to you, Zac?"

She heard the unsteadiness in her voice and cleared her throat. "You made it clear to him when he was here the other day that you're on my side. He won't forgive that. What if he refuses to see you?"

"Let me give it a try, sweetheart." His voice was velvet soft, gently compelling, weaving its usual magic as it curled through her. "We have a strong case. Getting rid of the vandal—the danger your father's so concerned about—isn't our only trump card."

His eyes caressed her, having the same soothing effect as his voice, calming her, mesmerizing her, crumbling her defenses.

"It isn't?"

"No. I want to tell your father that you and I are getting married."

"What?" Her eyes grew wide.

"Getting married. I love you, Rachel. I've loved you from the first moment I met you."

He reached for her then, gathering her in his arms and crushing her to his solid chest. She didn't resist. She couldn't. *Marriage…love…* It was like a dream. Did dreams ever come true?

But how could she think about love or dreams while the dark cloud of Mikey's custody hung over her?

Zac's hands ran gently up and down her arms, as if he felt her quivering. "You're a free woman now, Rachel, and we have a son together, and I want to bring him up as my son, even if you're not ready yet to acknowledge me publicly as Mikey's real father."

"Oh, Zac, I...I don't dare. Not right now, with my father..."

"We don't have to tell your father the truth about Mikey, simply that we're getting married. His grandson will have a mother *and* a father—the security of two parents—and Hedley will know you won't be alone anymore. You'll have my legal and personal protection. That should kill any thought of suing for custody."

She felt a dizzying flare of hope. But... "Mikey and I don't need anyone to *protect* us, Zac, now that we're rid of the vandal and the danger hanging over us." Besides, how could Zac promise to protect them into the future, when he had a life and a calling that would take him away eventually, married or not?

Because it *would.* He would never give up his work and the adventurous lifestyle he loved so much. Maybe for a time, but not forever.

"I know you don't need protecting, dearest, but it's another argument to throw at your father," he said. "The object is to get him to hand over Mikey—willingly." Zac's tone was unruffled, making her wonder if this whole talk of marriage and protection was simply a clever ploy on his part to get Mikey safely back. Was it? Would her father see through it?

Hope died as cold reality hit her. "But he *won't* hand him over, not willingly! My father never gives in. Not when he has his mind set on something."

And nothing meant more to him than having his daughter back in Sydney to follow in his footsteps at Barrington's. And one day, hopefully, his grandson to follow *her.*

"Just give me a chance, Rachel." Zac caught her face in his hands, forcing her to look at him. "We do have a good chance. You want to avoid having to fight for Mikey in the courts, don't you?"

"Of course I do!" She realized she was clinging to him. "I don't mean to be negative, but my father's never lost a fight in his life."

"He's never come up against me," Zac said, and she heard the same implacable, iron-hard intensity in his voice, the same unwavering self-confidence, that she'd heard so often in her father's.

She had a fleeting image of two powerful gladiators fighting to the death. Looking up at Zac, she felt a tremor, part admiration, part fear, quiver through her. Zac would make a worthy adversary, she had no doubt.

"I should leave now," Zac said, accepting her silence as a go-ahead. "It'll be dark soon. It'll take a few hours, so it'll be late by the time I get to Sydney. I'll grab an overnight bag in case your father won't see me until tomorrow."

She gulped at the reminder of his overnight bag. Would Zac sympathize with her if he knew she'd read her husband's gloating letter? Or would he be more worried that she might compare him to his mercenary twin brother?

As Zac steered her out into the hot afternoon sun to head back to the house, she brushed the memory aside to ask, "When my father calls back, should I tell him you're on your way to see him?"

"Why not? Tell him I've agreed to act as a go-between. That should encourage him to see me. He'll be hoping to talk *me* into what he wants, rather than the other way around."

Two indomitable gladiators, pitting their skills against each other.

Would Zac be a match for her father? She shivered, and as if feeling it, Zac lifted her hand and pressed it to his lips, sending a flow of heat into her veins. It made her long for this nightmare to be over so that he could kiss and savor the rest of her body, as well.

Would it ever happen? Nothing seemed certain anymore.

"You just stand firm, my angel," he murmured as he raised his head, leaving a moist, tingling imprint where his lips had burned into her hand. "Don't let your father bully you into giving in. Unless of course, you secretly *want* to go back to the city and run your father's company?"

His eyes held a teasing glint. She'd made it clear enough all along that it was the last thing she'd ever want.

"I don't. You know I don't. But if my father wins custody of Mikey..."

"He won't. I'll make him see that he wouldn't have a hope, that it would be futile for him to even try."

She felt a cold finger brush down her spine. Her father had never backed away from anything he'd wanted. Or failed in any fight he'd taken on. She just hoped Zac wasn't underestimating him...or overestimating his own capabilities. Her future depended on the outcome. *Their* future—hers and Mikey's and Zac's.

"Don't mention catching the vandal or getting married," Zac cautioned. "I want to surprise your father with our trump cards face-to-face. The two hitting him at the same time should knock the wind out of his sails."

"I hope so, Zac." But would her father have a trump card of his own up his sleeve?

She felt another shivery sensation and realized it was sweat trickling down her spine. This infernal hot weather! Would it never end? The continuing heat, the continuing lack of rain, did not augur well for the future.

Chapter Twelve

Watching Zac's plane rise into the clear blue sky, Rachel had to squint as the sharp rays of the late-afternoon sun turned the white metal into a dazzle of light. She hoped the sun in his eyes wouldn't dazzle Zac, as well. *Oh, Zac, keep safe. I'm relying on you.*

"If anyone can get your son back, Zac will," came a gruff voice from behind. It was Bazza.

She felt Buster's wet tongue licking her hand as she turned to probe the old man's bearded face, his sun-crinkled eyes. He wasn't just saying it to console her. He meant it, believed it. "You think a lot of Zac, don't you, Bazza." If they talked about Zac, it might help her not to think about Mikey.

"Zac's a great bloke. Everyone who knows him likes him."

"His twin brother didn't seem to like him much."
She dragged the words out. "Adrian never had a good
word to say about him. It…it made it hard for me to
trust Zac at first, or to know who the real Zac was."

Bazza scuffed his feet in the tough dry grass.
"Adrian had it in for Zac all his life. Blamed him for
their mum's death, which was stupid. She died giving
birth to Zac, half an hour after Adrian was born. But
it wasn't just that…." He hesitated, as if he felt he
was stepping onto dangerous ground. She was
Adrian's widow, after all.

"Tell me, Bazza, please. I'd like to know." She
forced her legs to move, wanting to get back to the
house before her father called. "We'll talk on the
way."

Bazza wheezed in a deep breath as he hobbled
alongside. "If you ask me, Adrian was jealous. Zac
was real bright, real outgoin', with lotsa friends. Always up to mischief and wantin' to try out new
things. Did real well at school. He was good at everythin' he did. But he never had tickets on himself."

"Go on," she prompted as he paused again.

"Adrian was more of a loner. The quiet, careful
type. Kept to himself. Hated books an' learnin'. Always wanted to be out in the paddocks, around the
cattle. Never had a lot of friends, never bothered…"
The old man hunched over, screwing up his face.
"But you don't wanna hear all this stuff. He was your
husband."

A husband who'd hidden things from her, hidden
his true colors.

"I don't think I knew my husband very well," she

said, sighing. "He didn't always tell me the truth, I suspect. Everything he told me about Zac was…well, I think he was just trying to make Zac look bad so I wouldn't like him or want to meet him."

And she hadn't wanted to. She'd believed everything her husband had told her. Until Zac had come back to stay and she'd soon seen a quite different side to him. And to her late husband, too.

"Adrian was forever telling lies an' runnin' Zac down to get him into trouble," Bazza said without looking at her. "Specially with their dad. Zac would just laugh or run off. He never hit back or held a grudge himself. Too busy enjoyin' life."

Rachel brushed a persistent fly from her face as she absorbed this latest insight into the twin brothers. Everything Bazza had told her rang true. She thought of her son, who'd thankfully inherited Zac's bold, adventurous spirit, his love of life, his boundless energy. She hoped it would help to keep his spirits up while he was away from her.

"Sounds as if Adrian had a real chip on his shoulder," she mused aloud. "He obviously resented his brother and hated being a twin."

She understood now why Adrian had never told her he had an identical twin brother, even getting rid of Zac's photographs and anyone around him who'd known his brother. He'd been afraid she would make comparisons. And she *had*. Zac was like a shining light and Adrian a pale glimmer. Poor Adrian. At least he'd never known…

"Y'know why everyone liked Zac?" There was genuine warmth in Bazza's gruff voice. "He cared about people, did things for people. He cared about animals an' birds an' everythin' under the sun.''

She'd come to see for herself that he did care. Deeply. Not only for people and birds and animals, but for the earth and the environment and the world in general.

Oh, Adrian, you just wanted me to despise your brother the way you did. Yet you secretly envied him, too. No wonder you never wanted me to meet him.

And with good reason, she thought soberly. She'd fallen under Zac's spell the first time she saw him, just like everyone else.

''Adrian never cared about those things?'' She hadn't seen much sign of it during their marriage.

Bazza's bony shoulders lifted and fell. ''All he cared about was the cattle station and ownin' it one day. All he ever wanted was Yarrah Downs.''

And marrying a girl who was going to inherit a fortune that he could lavish on his beloved property.

Her spirits flagged. And now Zac, his twin brother, had asked her to marry *him.*

''Zac's a good man, Rachel,'' Bazza said, as if reading her mind. ''You don't wanna take any notice of anythin' your husband told you. Trust your own eyes and what your heart tells you. Zac's as honest an' genuine as they come.''

''I know.'' She swallowed, regretting the way she'd lashed out at Zac in the past and feeling almost sorry for the man she'd married. From the day he'd first met her, Adrian had been afraid that she, like most people, would prefer his twin brother and wish that she'd married him, instead. That was why he hadn't wanted Zac at their wedding and why he'd been forever running Zac down.

She was glad she'd never told her husband that Zac had come back five years ago—come and gone the same night.

"You like Zac yerself, don'tcha, Rachel?"

Bazza's question jolted her back to earth. She drew in a deep breath to steady herself. "I... I..." She let her voice trail off, her eyes imploring Bazza to dispel her last doubts. He'd said the two brothers were nothing alike, but they *were* identical twins. What if they'd shared just one common trait? The prospect of untold wealth could seduce even the most noble and upright of men.

"You like Zac, but yer afraid he might be like your husband—chasin' after you for your money." Bazza's crinkled eyes were sympathetic.

She recoiled in shock. "How could you know my husband was after my money? You'd left Yarrah Downs before he even met me!"

Bazza shook his head. "I was with him the day he met you—at that rodeo at Longreach."

"You were there?" She pierced him with a sharp look. "I didn't see you."

"No, he made sure o' that. Didn't want me blabbin' to you that he already knew who you were."

She stared at him. "But Adrian didn't know who I was when we met that day. We only exchanged first names. He didn't find out who I was until after he'd proposed and I took him to meet my parents."

"Nah. He knew all right. Soon's he saw you he said, 'I've seen that girl before.' He'd seen you at the

Brisbane Royal Show the year before. You'd won a show jumping event an' everyone was talkin' about you, about how you were the daughter of Hedley Barrington an' heiress to the Barrington fortune.''

Rachel felt sick. *I fell for her,* Adrian had written in his letter to Zac, *before I found out who she was.*

So he'd even lied about that. And all this time she'd believed that he'd fallen for *her,* not for her name, not for her fortune. No wonder Adrian had swept her off her feet before she could draw breath. She'd often wondered about that, after she'd found out he wasn't the kind of man to act impulsively. She'd stupidly thought it must have been her fatal charm that had bowled him over. Ha!

''I don't recall seeing Adrian at the Brisbane show the day I won the show jumping,'' she said. She would have remembered him, surely. He'd been so tall and good-looking he would have really stood out. Like Zac...

''He didn't come near ya. Didn't think he had a chance with you back then. But when he saw you again at that Longreach rodeo—in the outback, like, in *his* world—he said he might stand a chance this time. He told me who you were without thinkin'. But he regretted it the minute he did.''

I bet he did. She felt chilled. *He wouldn't have wanted anyone knowing he was chasing after the Barrington heiress.* ''So he kept you away from me?''

''Better'n that, he sent me back to Yarrah Downs to pack my bags. Said it was time I retired. He'd never wanted me around, anyway. I knew too much about him. Knew what Zac was really like, too.''

She clasped the old man's bony shoulder. "It should never have happened, Bazza, sending you away. Zac was so upset when he found out. I'm so sorry."

"I'm not. I never wanted to work for Adrian, anyway. But I'd worked so long for his dad that this part o' Queensland was home, so I squatted in that old hut. Couldn't believe it when Zac turned up yesterday. But that's what he's like—he cares about ya. Money means nothin' to him, never did. He's nothin' like his brother."

"I—I know that, Bazza." She felt ashamed of the doubts she'd had. Where was Zac now? On his way to Sydney to fight for *her*...and for Mikey. And furthermore, risking her father's vengeance. If he'd been after Hedley Barrington's money, he would have been urging her to *bow* to her father's demands, not stand up to him.

"I'd give up my life for Zac." Bazza's gravelly voice cracked with emotion. "And I reckon he'd do the same for me. I know he'd give up his life for you." His small, black-currant eyes twinkled. "I seen the way he looks at you. An' I can see why. You're a real good woman, Rachel. Pretty, too."

She felt a blush rising. "I've been so unfair to Zac. I should have trusted him. All my instincts urged me to, but Adrian had told me such lies about him."

She blinked away a sting of tears. "I'll never doubt Zac again." *Or stop loving him, wanting him. Even if he doesn't stay in Australia indefinitely.*

But he'd talked about marriage, about being an equal partner. Had he meant it? If he did marry her, would he stay at Yarrah Downs or take off overseas again, and be an "equal partner" *in absentia?* Would she want a husband who was rarely at home?

Then she remembered Mikey. If Zac failed to talk her father out of suing for custody and he won, she'd be forced to give up her life here and go back to Sydney—or risk losing her son altogether. Would Zac still want to marry her if she and Mikey were living in Sydney?

Her head jerked up as the phone bell jangled from the veranda. Her heart gave an almighty thump. Her father? She broke into a run.

Her hands shook as she picked up the phone. "Rachel Hammond."

"Ah, Rachel, just a minute."

She opened and shut her mouth. How typical of her father to put her on hold!

"Hello, Mummy."

"Mikey!" She couldn't believe it. "Oh darling, it's so good to talk to you. How are you? What have you been doing?" She was careful not to ask if he was having a good time with his grandfather, afraid of what his answer might be.

"Mummy, Grandpa's house is so-o-o big! It's like a castle. He's gonna let me sleep upstairs in your old room. There's lots and lots of toys and a big rocking horse. Grandpa says I can have pizza for dinner."

She felt a squeezing hurt. Mikey sounded as if he was loving it there.

"Mummy, when are you coming? I want you here. Grandpa wants you to come, too."

He'd put Mikey up to this. "Oh, Mikey, I want to be with you, too." *But not in Sydney and certainly not at the Barrington fortress.*

"You see, Rachel?" Her father was back on the line. "You don't need to worry about your son. He's perfectly happy. He'd be even happier if you were here, too. But that's up to you."

In a wave of bitter anger and frustration, she lashed out at him with the first thing that came to mind. "You're feeding my son pizza?"

"It's the cook's night off. He *wanted* pizza. Rachel, I've given you time to consider. Have you come to a decision?" At least he didn't say "Come to your senses" this time. "I need you back here. I won't be able to work for much longer. I'm getting old and tired. I'm not well."

"What's wrong with you?" She was instantly suspicious. He'd always been as fit as a bull. If this was one of his cunning tricks, a play for sympathy...

"I've a heart problem. I mentioned it the other day."

And she hadn't believed him. Was it possible he *did* have heart trouble?

"I need to get my affairs in order." He paused. *For effect?* "My dear, I built up Barrington's for you, my only child, to carry on after me. It would break my heart to have to leave it to outsiders, to know there was no Barrington at the helm, no place for Mikey in the future, to have to hand it over to strangers rather than my family."

His voice, always so strong and implacable, actually shook. Which shook *her.* She could feel the net tightening again, the pressure building. Much as she still mistrusted him, his appeal touched her in a way she didn't expect. She actually found herself feeling sorry for him, felt her resistance faltering.

What if he was genuinely ill? To dash his last hope might literally break his heart. It might kill him. And she'd end up blaming herself for the rest of her life.

Stand firm, Zac had told her. But did she dare? It would be so easy if she knew her father's plaintive plea was simply a sly ruse to win her over. But what if it wasn't? What if he was in danger of a heart attack?

She must let him down lightly, appeal for his understanding.

"I know I've been a disappointment to you, Father. You wanted a son who would be like you and want the same things *you* want. I did try. I did the studies you wanted and had a stint at Barrington's, but it wasn't for me. I knew I had to live my own life. I'm sorry."

His voice rumbled back, gentle now, his usual aggression held in check. Maybe he realized that worked better than the bullying approach. "You have a son now, Rachel. Think of him. He'd have far more advantages and opportunities back here. Your lives would be so much easier. And safer. And richer. If you can't think of me, think of your son."

She stifled a moan. Maybe it *would* be best for Mikey. With the drought threatening to drive her off the land, how could she be sure she was even going to have a future at Yarrah Downs? The city might yet end up her only option. Would Barrington's lure her back then?

Her heart cried out in protest. She mustn't listen to him. Her father was clever enough, iron-willed enough, to try anything. She mustn't weaken, mustn't give in. *Stand firm,* Zac had said.

Zac. Her lionhearted gladiator, the man she loved, a rock of a man, who hadn't needed to think twice before rushing off to fight for her and Mikey.

The thought of Zac brought the blood coursing back into her veins. It straightened her spine, strengthened her resolve and put a glint back in her eye.

Zac would stand firm, no matter what Hedley Barrington threw at him. Even a multimillion-dollar bribe or the promise of endless riches eventually wouldn't sway Zac.

"Father, Zac's on his way to see you."

"Zac? Your brother-in-law? Well, well." Her father's tone was sardonic, and she knew he was thinking of Adrian and how easy it had been to manipulate and bribe *him.* Her father's initial bribe of a million dollars might have failed to tempt Adrian into dropping out of her life, but only because he'd seen a far greater prize in the offing if he held out and made a deal with her father.

Zac would never sink so low. He would never put money or Yarrah Downs before his family—before her and Mikey—the way Adrian had done. It shamed her to think that she'd ever believed he might. She and Mikey would always come first with Zac. Her father's money meant nothing to him. It was high time she realized that and laid her husband's ghost to rest.

"I've asked Zac to speak to you, Father, on my behalf," she said, trying to keep her voice steady, "before either of us takes any legal action." *Let him know he wasn't the only one making threats.*

"By all means, my dear. I've always believed in negotiation. Difficult matters can often be settled with reasonable debate."

Somehow her father made that sound like a threat, too. With a bit of bribery, did he mean? It sent a chill down her spine. Power and great wealth were dauntingly formidable weapons. Would Zac be strong enough to withstand them?

"When will your brother-in-law be here?" her father rapped out in a tone that suggested he was going to relish the confrontation.

Rachel's heart dipped further. "Not until late tonight. He's flying down in his Cessna. He'll call you when he gets to Sydney."

"I'll be waiting." The phone clicked in her ear.

She hadn't even had a chance to say good-night to Mikey.

It was the longest evening of her life. She worked out in the yards until dark, even escaping for a brief time for a short invigorating gallop on Silver, and afterward, when Vince and Joanne drove in from the paddocks, bringing them up-to-date on all that had happened and trying to pay attention as they gave an account of their day.

When it grew too dark to work outside, she settled

down in her painfully silent, still oppressively hot house, despite the fans, to tackle the station books.

An impossible task. She couldn't concentrate. All she could think about was Mikey, lapping up his grandfather's cushy lifestyle. And Zac, still in the air somewhere, flying in the dark, intent on the mission ahead.

She gave up on the books and trudged into the kitchen to bake some much-needed bread. She felt hotter than ever by the time it was ready, but at least it had given her something to do. Having skipped dinner, she bit into a hot crust, tempted by the enticing smell of freshly-baked bread. She could barely swallow it.

The evening dragged on. By now she was at fever pitch, her ears at full alert, waiting for the phone to ring, for Zac to report back. He must have landed in Sydney by now. Had he called her father yet?

If her father had invited Zac to come immediately, would Zac have rushed off without calling her first, not wanting to waste precious minutes?

The strain and the waiting were unbearable, leaving her so weary and emotionally exhausted she decided to take the portable phone into her bedroom and lie on her bed, beneath the overhead fan, to wait for Zac's call. Sleep was the furthest thing from her mind.

When the phone finally rang, she leaped so high she hit her head on the bedside lamp. "Hello? Is that you, Zac?"

"You were expecting another man to call at this hour?" he teased, but he quickly dropped the bantering note when she didn't respond. "Is something wrong, Rachel?"

Of course something was wrong! Her whole life, her whole future, hung in the balance! "Have you seen my father yet? Have you arranged a time to meet? Are you seeing him tonight? Where are you now? Tell me, Zac!"

"I've booked into the Hyde Park Inn. I hired a car at the airport. I've called your father and he says it's too late to meet tonight. He's agreed to meet me at three o'clock tomorrow—at his house."

"Not until midafternoon?" A groan dragged from her throat, erupting as an affronted growl. Her father was keeping Zac waiting deliberately. To increase the tension, to weaken his will, to make him putty in her father's hands!

Or to give her father time to speak to his lawyers before meeting Zac?

Her heart dropped to her toes. "You should have insisted on seeing him first thing in the morning!" she burst out.

"Your father has meetings all morning he can't put off." Zac sounded infuriatingly unruffled. He ought to be seething at having to wait. "He's brought back your old nanny, he told me, to look after Mikey."

"My old…" Oh, this was the last straw! Her old nanny had been like a prison warden, a sour-faced, gimlet-eyed watchdog! Mikey would hate her. "He should be with *me*, not with a nanny!"

"I agree, my love. And he will be, I promise."

But when? she cried silently. *When she agreed to go back to Sydney?*

"I'm so worried, Zac," she moaned. "How can you sound so calm?"

"Years of practice, stalking elusive wildlife," came the smooth reply. "What are you doing right now, my darling?"

"Me? Right now?" What did it matter what she was doing? Only Mikey mattered! "I'm lying on my bed, going slowly crazy," she told him, her tone caustic. "Why?"

"That's exactly what I was about to tell you to do, my darling. Go to bed."

"Oh, you were, were you? To do what? To drift off into sweet, unworried dreams? I'll never sleep! I'm too uptight."

"Precisely why I want you lying in bed. So I can help you to relax."

Her heart gave a tiny jump. "Just what did you have in mind? Hypnotism over the phone? Mind suggestion?"

"If you want to call it that." His voice dropped to a low, sensual purr. "I prefer to call it giving in to a feast of sensation…feelings…scents…touch…soft words. Lie back and let the feast flow over you, my sweet. Imagine I'm there with you…loving you…."

"Oh Zac, I wish you *were* here!" She could feel a heightened awareness already, an increase in her heart rate, a spreading sweetness in her limbs. Was that what he meant by a "feast of sensation"?

"I *am* there, my darling, right beside you. Now lie back…don't talk…just listen…and feel…let your senses take flight…."

Intrigued, she sank back on the pillows, holding the

phone close to her ear, her already heated body sprawled out on the sheet, every nerve end tingling in anticipation.

Zac's voice was a soothing murmur in her ear. "Imagine the soft whir of the fan overhead...the sharp, monotonous chirps of the cicadas outside. The air is heavy with the scent of roses drifting in from the garden..."

The air she'd thought so hot and cloying miraculously sweetened as his words wove their magic.

"Your hair is tumbling over the pillows like a golden waterfall..."

"Zac," she murmured, "you could write romantic novels!"

"Hush. Just listen and feel. Imagine my fingers running through your hair...my lips buried in the silken strands... Mmm, it smells so sweet, like wildflowers or fresh hay. It feels so soft under my lips...."

She moaned, as if his lips actually were in her hair.

"I'm sliding my hands over your white satin nightgown, over the warm soft curves underneath...."

She sighed dreamily, her old cotton nightie magically transformed into sensuous white satin.

"My fingers are tingling, impatient to feel the softness of naked skin. They grasp the white satin and drag it upward...."

Her pulse quickened.

"Aah. The sight of you, lying naked under my gaze! Feel my hands gliding over your silken skin, over your smooth, flat stomach, your ribs, your breasts...." His voice thickened.

She could feel her breasts tingling, tightening.

"My hot gaze is burning into their creamy perfection...the rosy peaks spring to life...."

Her nipples hardened.

"I have an overwhelming urge to touch those lush buds, to feel them under my fingers, to bring my mouth down and drink in their sweetness...."

She gave a moan. It was as if his hands were actually on her, moving sensually over her exposed breasts, kneading, sliding, squeezing, as if his lips were grazing over her straining flesh, his tongue doing an erotic dance on a sensitive peak before his lips took over, sucking deeply... Her heart thumped erratically.

"My hand is moving lower."

Her body began to ache and throb.

"I'm stroking your thighs, stroking the special place between...." Rachel's body was on fire, damp with sweat, squirming with her need for him.

"Oh God, Rachel, the thought of you is driving me crazy!" Zac's agonized groan dissolved the magical spell he'd been weaving.

"Oh, Zac, I want you so much!" she cried, pressing the phone to her ear, as if that would bring him closer.

"Darling, I'm sorry." She could hear his heavy breathing, hear the huskiness in his voice. "I was trying to relax you, put you in the mood for sleep, not arouse you...or myself, damn it!"

"Zac, you *have* relaxed me—unbelievably." It was true. He'd given her something else to think about, to feel, to savor, to help take her mind off Mikey. "It's as if you're here with me, holding me, loving me, kissing my worries away. And we *will* be together, Zac, soon. I know we will. I feel so much more hopeful now, and sure about…about everything.''

"We'll all be together soon, Rachel, the three of us—you and Mikey and me. Just hold on to that thought.''

"I will, Zac,'' she promised. "You'll call me tomorrow as soon as you've seen my father? Whatever happens?''

"As soon as I can, my darling. Make sure you're home around three-thirty, four o'clock. I should know something by then. Spend the day out in the paddocks with Vince and Joanne, or take a long horseback ride. No need to stay by the phone. I've some business to do myself in the morning.''

Business in Sydney? What business? she wondered. The investments he'd mentioned once? "Let me know as soon as you can, Zac.'' She made a kissing sound into the phone. "That kiss was for you, my darling. Thank you…for tonight. I think I might even be able to sleep now.''

"Then sleep, my darling, and sweet dreams. Dream of me, if you can arrange it. I know I'll be dreaming of you.''

"I've been dreaming of you, Zac, for the past five years,'' she confessed. "I can't see tonight being any different with your feast of sensation still fresh in my mind.'' *In my mind, heart, body and soul.*

"I'll make your dreams come true, Rachel. Believe it.''

''I can believe anything of you, Zac,'' she said. And right now she did.

Her beloved, intrepid gladiator would triumph over her father. He had to!

Chapter Thirteen

Rachel awoke to a blood red sky. It was spectacular. She'd never seen anything like it. Was it a warning, a sign of a change in the weather at last? She hardly dared hope.

Her spirits dipped when she stepped outside to feed the horses and saw that the sky was still clear, an endless expanse of pale, unbroken blue, with only a few tiny white puffs of cloud on the far horizon. They'd probably be gone in an hour or two.

Vince and Joanne were preparing to leave in the Land Rover to check the fences and any loosened posts, a constant job.

"I'll ride out and help you when I've finished here in the yards," she said. Some hard riding and tough physical work might help to keep her mind off Mikey, and off Zac's meeting this afternoon with her father.

At eight o'clock that morning, Zac pulled up in the rental car outside the massive gates of the Barrington mansion. He announced himself and drove through as the gates swung open, following a sweeping driveway lined with graceful silver birches.

He hoped Rachel would understand, when he got home, why he'd told her he wasn't seeing her father until three o'clock. He'd wanted to give himself time to get back to Yarrah Downs by midafternoon, around the time she'd be expecting his call, so that he could report back to her in person, not over the phone. Good or bad news, he wanted to be with her when she heard.

Her father *had* suggested meeting later in the day, but Zac had put his foot down, adamant that they must meet first thing in the morning, no matter how early. He'd won that battle, at least.

He could hear dogs barking, but they'd obviously been chained up to allow his safe approach. He left the car in a parking bay close to the imposing mansion and walked through a grand portico, between towering columns, to the front door.

To his surprise Barrington answered the door himself, though shadowy figures were visible in a far corner of the grand entrance hall. Bodyguards? Servants? There was no sign of Mikey. No sound, either, which was unlike his exuberant son.

"Ah, Zac. Good to see you." Barrington smiled as he thrust out a hand.

The smile on the face of a tiger? "Mr. Barrington." Zac accepted the offered hand with the merest smile of his own. *He's hoping I'll be a pushover, a pawn, like my twin brother.* "Where's Mikey?" he demanded.

"Hedley, please. My grandson's playing in the rear courtyard with his nanny and the pedal car Rachel had as a child. You can see him after we've had our chat." He ushered Zac into a large, book-lined study. "We'll talk in here." He waved Zac to a leather armchair, choosing the chair behind the desk for himself.

Zac made no move to sit down. He waited for Rachel's father to settle before stepping forward and leaning over the desk, placing his hands flat on the polished surface. He made no attempt to hide the dark, dangerous gleam in his eye.

"I ought to knock your lights out, Hedley, for what you've done to your daughter." His voice was soft but edged with steel. "You don't deserve to see her ever again. Or your grandson, either."

Barrington's eyes barely flickered, a supercilious curl lifting his lip. "It was for my daughter's own safety and well-being that I took Mikey away from her. To bring her to her senses."

"To bend her to your will, you mean." Zac's face hardened. "But I'm not talking about your abduction of Mikey. I'm talking about the vandalism you ordered your paid lackey, Danny, to carry out."

Barrington went still, his sharp eyes narrowing. "What the hell are you—"

"Read this!" Zac thrust a folded note at him. It was a copy of the signed confession, incriminating

Rachel's father, that he'd extracted from Danny before letting him "escape."

Barrington unfolded it, read a few lines and gave a snort. But Zac noted how his neck swelled and reddened. It had hit home all right. But unlike Danny, he wasn't a man to easily cave in. "Who's going to believe this?"

"Your *daughter* would believe it," Zac rasped. "And it would be the last time you ever saw or heard from her. Is that what you want? To lose your daughter *and* your grandson? To never see them again?"

Barrington pursed his lips. "You're saying Rachel doesn't know about these lies against me? You haven't told her? Haven't shown her this worthless piece of paper?"

"They're not lies, Hedley, and you know it. And, no, I haven't told her yet. She only knows that Danny's the vandal and that he's escaped. But I'll show her his confession if you force me into it. Can you imagine how she'd take it? Her own father, paying her jackaroo to vandalize her property! Her own father, trying to ruin her!"

As Barrington sucked in an enraged breath, Zac thrust his face closer. "Makes a mockery of your custody threats, doesn't it, Hedley? You claim Rachel's not safe at Yarrah Downs, but she's not safe because of *you*. *You're* the one who should be facing the law!"

"That libelous confession would never stand up in a court of law," Barrington scoffed. "It would never even *get* that far. Danny would never testify against me. You've no real proof against me!"

The man was worried, Zac was certain. "Your respective satellite-phone records should be damning enough," he drawled. "And I'm sure the media would have a field day with Danny's signed confession, proved or not. Your reputation would be in tatters. But it's your daughter you should be most worried about. She wouldn't need any proof. She'd *know* it's the truth. And hate you for it."

As Barrington's chest heaved and fell, Zac remembered his other trump card and swooped in for the kill. "I intend to marry your daughter, Hedley, and bring up Mikey as my own son—at Yarrah Downs, where they both want to be. You can forget about suing for custody. Mikey will have a loving mother *and* a father to look after him!"

Barrington's big hands clenched into fists, his mouth lifting in scorn. "You're a wildlife photographer, not a cattleman. You won't stay in Australia!"

"I *was* a wildlife photographer. When I was unattached, with no woman or family of my own to keep me in one place. Now I have, and I intend to settle down with Rachel and raise Mikey as she wants him to be raised. They'll be safe with me. They certainly haven't been safe with *you*."

Barrington abruptly dropped all pretense. "I gave strict orders that nothing that worthless jackaroo did was to hurt my family in any way. I would never let anyone harm a hair on their heads!"

"You think Rachel hasn't been hurt? Imagine how she's been feeling all these weeks, with an unknown hooligan vandalizing her property, causing her untold worry and expense. Imagine how she's been suffering since you snatched Mikey, with your custody threat hanging over her.''

"Everything I did was for her own good!'' Barrington's massive body shook with emotion. "She belongs in the city, in the world she grew up in and the business I trained her for. It's her *heritage*. Her son's heritage. Her husband agreed that she should come back to Sydney when I needed her. Your own twin brother! What makes *you* any different?''

Scorn curled Zac's lip. "My brother only cared about your money and what it would do for Yarrah Downs. I only care about Rachel and Mikey and what *they* want. They want the life they have at the station and they want *me*. They don't want Barrington's and they don't want your money! Face it, Hedley. Rachel's never coming back!''

Barrington's eyes gleamed with a sudden reckless cunning. "You're saying that if I offered you ten million dollars to bring her back to Barrington's, you'd turn it down? I offer it now. Final offer!''

Zac's eyes burned into the older man's. "You could offer me your entire fortune, Hedley, and I'd still turn it down. Unlike my twin brother, I don't want a bar of your money, now or ever.''

"Is that so? Well, I swear to you, if my daughter's serious about not coming back, I'll sell Barrington's and neither of you will get a cent—ever. I'll set up a trust for my grandson, but the rest will go into a special foundation. All that money will go to worthy causes and charities, none to you or my daughter!''

"An excellent idea, Hedley. Your daughter would applaud it, too.''

"Good," Barrington growled, but he sounded defeated. "You mean it, don't you. Rachel's not coming back. She doesn't want Barrington's and she doesn't want anything else from me."

"No. But she still might want you as a father. As Mikey's grandfather. That's why I haven't told her Danny was working for you or shown her his confession. Do you want to remain a part of your daughter's life and see your grandson occasionally?"

Hedley's face twitched. "Of course I do. They're all I have."

"Then agree to stop interfering in her life and making futile demands on her, and I'll keep quiet about your involvement with Danny—and let you go on seeing your daughter and grandson. I can still show Rachel his confession if I have to." He let the threat hang in the air.

Barrington was no fool. He knew he was beaten, that he had no room to argue or maneuver. Zac was offering him a way out, a face saver, a slender ray of light. He was offering Hedley his family back—but on his, Zac's, terms.

Zac leaned closer. "If you want your daughter to be happy, Hedley, you'll let her live her life the way she wants to. She'd be desperately unhappy in the city. Is that what you'd want—to see her unhappy?"

"No. Of course not." Barrington heaved a sigh. "All right, I agree," he said, a glimmer of respect in his eyes. He might have lost Rachel as a successor to his business empire, but he was plainly determined not to lose her as a daughter or to see her desperately unhappy. "I suppose I ought to be grateful to you for wanting to save my relationship with my daughter and grandson,'' he muttered. ''And you've satisfied me you're doing it for their sakes, not for mercenary reasons of your own.''

He squinted at Zac from under his heavy brows. ''You're a different man from your brother.'' The admission came slowly. ''You seem to genuinely care for Rachel—enough to put her first, not the money she may inherit one day.''

Zac recoiled. ''I meant what I said, Hedley. Neither of us wants your money. We'll thrive at Yarrah Downs from now on, without your destructive interference, or Danny's.''

Wincing, Barrington made a further grudging admission. ''I'm sure you'll look after my daughter and grandson, even if it isn't the life I've always wanted for them.''

''I will, Hedley. You can be very sure of that.''

Barrington gave him a long, assessing look. ''I think Rachel will be happier with you than she was with your brother. I always had the feeling she wanted more from Adrian. That's why I thought I had a chance of getting her back—especially when he left her a widow.''

The hard lines of Zac's face softened a trifle. ''You're welcome to come and visit us, Hedley, as a father and grandparent. As long as you stick to the rules and never mention Barrington's or selling Yarrah Downs again.''

''There won't *be* a Barrington's. I meant what I said about selling the business and setting up a charitable foundation. My doctors tell me my heart's not the best and I should slow down.'' His shoulders hunched. Suddenly he looked his age. ''Taking Mikey was crazy, the last act of a desperate man. Tell Rachel I'm sorry. Deeply sorry. And give her my blessing. You both have it.''

''Thank you, Hedley.'' Zac smiled, genuinely, for the first time. ''I hope your new venture works out. Now, may I see Mikey?''

The old man sighed, resigned, to losing his greatest battle. ''Of course. Follow me.''

Rachel rode back to the homestead just before three. By now, amazingly, those tiny white clouds covered the entire sky, and a slight breeze had sprung up, dropping the temperature by a few welcome degrees. But whether this subtle change in the weather would lead to rain was anybody's guess.

The waiting was torture, but she was determined not to mope around worrying. To keep her mind off Mikey and Zac, she threw herself into some vigorous housework.

As she was cleaning the kitchen oven later, she heard a sound she wasn't expecting. A light plane was flying overhead!

Zac? She glanced at her watch. Zac couldn't possibly be back. It was only four o'clock! He was supposed to be calling her from Sydney around four o'clock!

She ran out onto the veranda, just in time to see a familiar white Cessna disappear below the trees. It *was* Zac's plane. And it was coming in to land.

She started running, a terrible fear gripping her.

Her father must have changed his mind about meeting Zac. He must have called Zac early to cancel their afternoon meeting, refusing for some reason to see him at all.

Had Zac had a chance to tell her father they'd disposed of the danger from the vandal? And that they planned to marry? Had her father managed somehow to trump *Zac's* trump cards? Why else would Zac have given up and come home?

Oh Zac! She knew how failure, how having to admit defeat, not being able to help their son and not being able to help her, would make him feel.

She saw Bazza working in the yard but didn't stop. He would have heard Zac's plane, too, and know where she was heading. She dimly noted as she ran that the white clouds had merged into a pale-gray blanket overhead. A darker bank of cloud hung low over the distant hills.

Rain clouds?

If it rained, really rained this time, enough to break the drought, it would be painfully ironic. She might have to leave here soon. If her father had refused to give up Mikey, if he won custody of her son, she would have no alternative.

She wasn't even sure she cared anymore. She only cared about being reunited with her son.

Through the trees she glimpsed the airstrip ahead, Zac's plane sitting on the tarmac. She strained her eyes for her first glimpse of his familiar swinging gait, his dark, tussled hair, his wide, powerful shoulders. If his rescue mission had failed he'd doubtless be in need of comfort himself...

And then she saw a mirage. It had to be a mirage. Her mind had conjured up Mikey, skipping ahead of Zac, waving his small arms as he saw her emerge from the trees, his familiar, high-pitched squeals of laughter echoing across the heavy, humid distance between them.

She gave a yelp of joy and relief and flew across the scorched grass to meet him.

Mikey flung himself into her arms. "Mummy, Mummy! I flew in Uncle Zac's plane and in Grandpa's jet and I slept in Grandpa's castle! But I wished *you* were there, Mummy. And Buster. And Rocky. And Uncle Zac. And everybody!"

"Oh, Mikey!" She kissed him all over his small, glowing face, almost drowning him in her tears, her hands savoring the feel of him under her fingers. "I'm so glad you're home. I've missed you so much!"

Mikey pulled back, wiping his mother's tears from his plump cheeks with the back of his hand. "Why are you crying, Mummy? I missed you, too." Suddenly he looked a bit stricken. "Grandpa said it was all right to go wif him. He said I'd like it at his house, but I didn't. He didn't even let me play wif his dogs. And a nasty lady bossed me around."

"Never mind, darling, you're home now."

"Yeah!" Mikey tossed his head, his dark hair flopping, just like Zac's, his lively gray eyes—Zac's eyes—drinking in the dusty yards, the golden paddocks, the rustling gum trees, the wide-open spaces. "I like it much, much better here! Where's Buster?"

"Oh, dear!" She'd shut Buster in the laundry while she was cleaning the oven. He must still be there, probably sound asleep. "He's in the house, darling, out of the heat."

"I wanna see him!" Mikey cried. "An' can I have something to eat, Mummy? I'm starving. We ____ outta food. Can I have a ride on Rocky after?"

She laughed. Mikey was back home with a vengeance!

"Now that you're back home, my darling, you can have whatever you like," she promised him, her eyes seeking Zac's as he hovered behind. Her rapturous gaze held his for an endless moment. "Thank you, Zac," she whispered. "I can't believe you're back so soon. How did you manage it?"

"I talked your father into meeting me early this morning. I didn't call because I wanted to surprise you."

Or be back here with her if the news was bad? She let her eyes cling to his, showing him she understood and loved him for being the kind of man he was. She only broke eye contact when Mikey tugged at her hand.

"Come on, Mummy!"

"Yes, darling." As Mikey dragged her away, she glanced back. "Are you coming, Zac?"

"Later. I'll tell you everything tonight, when we're alone," he said, his eyes promising other, more-intimate delights, as well. "You go and spend some time with your son. I'll bring Bazza up-to-date, and Vince and Joanne when they get back. Don't bother about dinner for me. I'll be in to grab a snack shortly. You concentrate on Mikey."

Her lively son kept her on the run for the rest of

the afternoon, and she caught only tantalizing glimpses of Zac, once when he popped into the house to grab a cool drink and a hunk of bread and cheese, and another time when she was giving Mikey a ride on Rocky and saw Zac talking to Vince and Joanne, who'd just arrived back.

Her pulse leaped each time she saw him, each time she thought of him…and the night ahead. And whenever she looked at her precious son, back home where he belonged, she was convinced her heart would burst with happiness. She had them both back again, the two people she loved most in the world.

The sky had darkened even further, the clouds a thick, murky black now, low and threatening over the dry paddocks. Dared she hope for some real rain at last? As lightning flashed over the far hills, followed by a rumble of thunder, she crossed her fingers.

"Better go in now, Mikey." She didn't want him out in the open when there was lightning. "Time for tea and a bath."

By the time her son had filled his tummy, washed his grime off in the bath and put on his pajamas, he was almost falling asleep on his feet. But he refused to go to bed until Zac came in and said good-night.

She felt a flutter of unease, wondering what conditions her father had made before handing over Mikey, and if he was still hoping that she…

She squeezed her eyes shut for a dark, foreboding second. Her father was a fiercely determined, implacable man. She couldn't see him giving up on the dream he'd had for so long—to have his daughter following in his footsteps at Barrington's. The danger from the vandal might have gone, but her father would still insist that she wasn't safe at Yarrah Downs, that she wouldn't have Zac here forever, even if he married her.

And Zac probably *would* get itchy feet after a while and want to go off into the wilds again, leaving her alone for extended periods. He'd been a wildlife photographer for so long, an adventurous free spirit for so long. The lure and excitement of that kind of life must be in his blood.

She let out a trembling sigh. She desperately wanted Zac here with her now, not only to thank him again for bringing Mikey home, however he'd managed it, but because her body was crying out for him.

She could feel her heartbeat fluttering already at the thought of being in his arms again, spending the whole night with him. Because this time it was going to happen. Nothing was going to stop them. Tonight would be theirs and theirs alone.

She wouldn't let the specter of her father spoil it. Nothing would spoil this special night.

The house lit up with a blinding flash, and an explosive crack of thunder rocked the house. She laughed aloud, prepared to challenge the elements. *Go on, knock out the power, start a bushfire, split our eardrums, I don't care. Nothing will stop us tonight!*

Mikey, following her lead, gave a squeal of laughter. "I'm not scared, either, Mummy. It's only a silly old storm."

She hugged him. "That's right, pet, but we're safe in here."

Safe.

Yes, she had her precious son safely home again. And she had Zac to thank, for exposing Danny and triumphing over her father, somehow persuading him to back down and hand over his grandson.

"Darling, let's get you into bed. I'll read you a story while we wait for Uncle Zac." She wouldn't be able to concentrate on a single word, but reading aloud might stop her from going crazy.

After tucking Mikey in, she snuggled down beside him and started reading one of his favorites, *Green Eggs and Ham,* until a thunderous roar drowned out her voice. Mikey's head jerked up. "What's that noise?" He had to bellow, his small, high voice barely audible over the din.

A smile burst across Rachel's face. She heard herself laughing aloud again. "It's rain, Mikey. Pouring rain!" Rain such as she hadn't heard in years and thought she'd never hear again. Steady, solid rain that would be thudding into the parched earth and, if it kept up like this for long enough, soaking deep.

She seized Mikey in her arms and rocked him from side to side. "Keep on pouring, rain!" she cried. "Keep on pouring like this for days and days!"

Mikey giggled, then gasped, "Mummy, I can't breathe! You're squeezing me too tight."

"Sorry, darling." She drew back to see Zac standing over the bed, grinning at them. His hair was wet, sticking out in dark spikes, his damp shirt clinging to the solid muscles of his arms and chest. Never had he looked so magnificent, so strong, so loving, so perfect.

A whoosh of joy and a flaming, delicious weakness

swept through her, right down to the pit of her stomach, a sweetness that flowed into her limbs and veins and warmed her soul. She loved him so much. Loved and wanted him.

"Zac! I didn't hear you come in."

Chapter Fourteen

"Uncle Zac!" Mikey flung out his small arms. "It's waining! It's pouring cats and dogs! Will the dams fill up now?"

Zac folded them both in the solid warmth of his arms, clasping them to his sodden shirt. Nobody cared about the dampness or the drops of water that splashed from his hair.

"I sure hope so, Mikey." His eyes, under lashes still glistening from the rain, sought and found Rachel's. "A true outback son," he said with a nod of approval.

"I want to be *your* son, too, not just Mummy's, Uncle Zac." Mikey looked up at Zac with big, solemn eyes. "I want you to be my daddy. I don't have a daddy anymore. Can I call you Daddy, Uncle Zac?"

"Well, if your mummy will marry me I *will* be your daddy," Zac murmured, his eyes still holding Rachel's captive. "How about you go to sleep now, tiger, so I can ask her?"

"Ask her now!" Mikey cried. "Say yes, Mummy! Say you'll marry Uncle Zac!"

Rachel's eyes misted. It was what she wanted, wasn't it? To marry Zac and love and cherish him forever—wherever he might be? Even a few weeks with Zac at a time, or even a few days or a few hours, would be better than not having him at all. He was Mikey's real father, more of a father already than Adrian had ever been. And he loved her.

But there was still her father. Her lip trembled. Zac hadn't told her yet what demands her father had made before handing over Mikey.

"A marriage proposal is something for two people to do in private, Mikey." Zac's voice rumbled above her like velvet. Perhaps he'd noted her hesitation, sensed something still niggled at her. "You'll have to go to sleep now, tiger, so I can ask her. But I'm hoping, by the time you wake up tomorrow, you'll be able to start calling me Daddy."

The easy confidence in his voice lifted her spirits. Zac would make things come right. He always did. He'd shown that he loved her, that he loved Mikey. And she loved and trusted him. Nothing else mattered.

Mikey's mouth stretched in a satisfied grin as he flopped back onto the pillows. Zac dropped a kiss on his tussled hair and stepped back. "Off to sleep now, tiger, okay? Your mother and I need to talk." *Among other things,* his smoldering eyes told Rachel.

Any lingering qualms slipped away. In a moment she would be in his arms where she belonged, where she would always belong. "Good night, Mikey darling." She gave her son a warm hug and rose, too, her eyes glowing, spirits floating. "Sleep tight, my pet."

"Good night, Mummy. Good night, Daddy." Mikey sounded drowsily content. And every bit as confident as his father. There was no way he was going to wait until the morning to start calling Zac *Daddy.*

Blissfully alone at last! And the rain was still falling—steady, soaking rain, filling the leaf-clogged gutters and noisily overflowing, sending water tumbling down the pipes and windows. At any other time Rachel might have rushed outside to clear the drains, but not tonight. If there was a flood out in the yards, Vince and Joanne could deal with it. Or Bazza. She could rely on all three of them.

She moved into Zac's arms, just as the grandfather clock in the lounge began to chime eight. She had the dreamy feeling it was chiming for *them,* announcing, *It's time for Rachel and Zac.*

"I knew you'd bring Mikey home, if anyone could," she murmured, quivering as she felt his heartbeat against hers. It was as erratic as her own.

Suddenly it didn't seem important to know the details of his meeting with her father, or to hear what her father might have said or threatened to do. All

that mattered to her at this moment was Zac, and being alone with him at last, just the two of them.

Zac's hand slid up her back to the nape of her neck,
his fingers tangling in her hair, long since loosened
from the braid she'd clawed at in the anguish of waiting for news of Mikey.

"I told your father I intend to marry you, my darling, and help you run Yarrah Downs. So make an
honest man of me and say yes!"

"Oh, Zac, it's what I want more than anything,
but—"

He groaned. "Oh please. No buts."

"But I *know* my father." Despite her aching need
for Zac and her vow not to think about her father, her
fears swirled back. "He won't give in. He'll try something else. He'd do anything to make me come back
to Barrington's."

Zac hushed her with his lips. "But he *has* given
in, my love. He knows it's all over."

As she looked up at him in wonder, she felt his
other hand moving over her lower back, making it
hard for her to think of anything but him.

"Can we forget about your father for tonight?" His
hips were nudging hers, letting her feel another more
intimate part of him, a hard, highly potent part of him
that dissolved her insides and sent logical thought to
the four winds. "I'm trying to propose to you. And
after that, I intend to make love to you…slowly and
thoroughly, and to keep making love to you all night
long."

All night long. The very prospect made her dizzy.

She'd waited so long for this moment, dreamed about it for so long.

"Oh, Zac…" No other words came. Her body was already on fire, her breath coming in little gasps, her skin tingling with the need for more intimate contact. How could she concentrate on a formal marriage proposal when all she wanted was Zac's mouth smothering hers, his hands caressing her bare skin, his heated body on hers?

She gazed up at him with expectant eyes, already glazed with her hunger for him.

"I love you, Rachel. I want to marry you." He groaned the words against her eager lips. "If you love me, say yes, my darling, and say it quickly. I'm aching to make love to you." His hand was on the swell of her buttock now, pressing her into him. "*Will* you?"

She arched and cried out, hot flames igniting her body, scorching her veins. "Yes!" It was both an answer and a plea. "I'll marry you, Zac! I love you. I'll always love you, wherever you are and whatever happens in the future."

She dragged him across the room, afraid that in another second she'd be too weak to move. "Take me to your bedroom, Zac!"

"*My* bedroom?"

"Yes!" Mindless as she felt, she could still think enough to know that she didn't want to make love to him in the master bedroom, in the bed she'd shared with her husband. She didn't want any reminders of Adrian. Before sharing that room with Zac, she would redecorate and replace the bed, wiping out all trace of her previous marriage.

"With the utmost pleasure." With a husky growl, Zac swung her up in his arms, just as he had on the night of the fire. Only this time there was no fire, no power failure, nothing to disrupt the spellbinding mood.

By the time they reached Zac's bed, they were kissing and tearing at their clothes in frantic longing, not caring about popped buttons or ripped seams.

Within seconds they were both naked, their heated bodies glistening with sweat in the muted glow of the bedside lamp. They feasted on the sight of each other, before the impact of skin on skin brought gasps of even greater need.

The long, frustrated years since they'd first clung in a naked embrace rolled away, and the fantasy dreams that had haunted their sleep since scattered into fairy dust.

Nothing matched the reality. Zac swept her to places she'd never dreamed of, igniting new and erotic sensations that blew her mind and flooded her whole being in a spiraling wave of passion.

At the earth-shattering moment of release, a heart-felt cry was dragged from her throat, just as it had been five years ago. "I love you! I love you with all my heart!" Only this time she knew it was Zac, not Adrian, making love to her, and he was not just *making* love to her but *loving* her in a way Adrian never had or could.

Over the next few hours he made her feel those glorious sensations again and again, more blissfully each time, his own powerful skills and responses blowing her mind even more.

The rain—the kind of steady rain they needed so badly—was still coming down as the first rays of dawn crept into Zac's bedroom. They lay on the bed beneath a thin sheet, finally asleep, both still bathed in sweat and enveloped in the warmth of their love for each other.

It was where Mikey found them, waking them far too soon by clambering onto the bed and flopping down between them.

"Mummy, I've been looking for you! Daddy, wake up! It's morning. Mummy, did you say yes?"

Rachel struggled to open her eyes. She felt no embarrassment at being found in Zac's bed by her young son. She would never again feel embarrassed to be with Zac.

"Yes, my darling, I did say yes. Zac and I are going to get married." The reality of saying the words, and what they meant, chased sleep away. Had her father truly given up on his longtime dream for her and accepted that she was going to marry Zac and stay on here at Yarrah Downs, or had Zac been too optimistic?

A slither of unease coiled through her. It was something her father had expected and longed for from the moment she was old enough to understand, and he'd kept on wanting it even after she'd married Adrian. Since her husband's death, he'd become even more obsessive about bringing her back to Sydney, back to Barrington's.

He must have reached desperation point to have

taken such an extreme measure—kidnapping his grandson!—to force her to come back.

"Mikey, go and get dressed," she said, giving her beaming son a hug, "and then you can run out and tell Buster and Rocky that your mummy is going to marry your uncle Zac."

She no longer feared kidnappers or deliberately lit fires or other dangers. Danny had run for his life—a vandal with a conscience. He must have felt a stab of guilt to have left her his uncle's bribe money!

Yes. Her family was safe now. Besides, Bazza and Vince and Joanne would be out in the yards this morning to keep an eye on her precious son. "We'll be out in a minute, darling."

Never one to stay still for long, Mikey wriggled off the bed. "I'll tell 'em, Mummy. See you, Daddy!" With a happy squawk he scooted off.

"Now—" Zac pulled her back into his arms, looking down at her with tender, perceptive eyes "—what is it, my darling? You're not still worried about your father, are you?"

How well he knew her! "I just can't see him giving up. Even if you marry me, he'll still try to—"

"No, he won't." Zac smiled, as confident as ever. "He's finally accepted that your future is with me, not with Barrington's, that you don't want that kind of life and never will. I've satisfied him that you and Mikey come first in my life and that I'll always be around to take care of you both."

"Oh, Zac, you don't have to take care of us or give up your career for us! Now that Danny and his uncle are out of our lives, there's no one threatening us anymore. And if this rain continues and it ends the drought…'' She clung to him, realizing what it would mean. Water in the troughs and dams, feed for the cattle, strong, healthy stock again. The future of Yarrah Downs looked suddenly brighter.

"I know how you love your wildlife photography, Zac.'' She wound her arm round his neck and rested her cheek against his rough jaw. "If you want to go off to do your Australian assignment, or go on overseas assignments in the future…wherever you want to go, Zac—''

"Rachel, my love, you're not listening to me. I want to be your life partner, not only in marriage, but in our lives, in everything. Wherever you and Mikey are, I intend to be. Here. In Timbuktu. Even in the city, if you want to go back eventually, for Mikey's sake. I'd follow you anywhere. I've given up the life I had before—without any regrets.''

Given it up. Her heart soared. "You think a cattle station will have sufficient challenges for an adventurous wildlife expert like you?''

He smiled, a heart-stopping smile that she saw reflected in the silver-gray of his eyes and that held no doubts whatsoever. "We have plenty of challenges here. Once things pick up a bit, we could even consider opening the place to tourists, as others have done, offering first-class meals and accommodation, and inviting people from the cities and overseas to taste life on a working cattle station.''

"You mean, build special accommodation for paying guests? Like a motel?''

"Why not? We'd only need enough rooms for a

few couples at a time. You and I could act as hosts, taking our guests out mustering and drafting and viewing the wildlife, with extra staff to help with meals and cleaning. If we make it exclusive enough and interesting enough, tourists will flock here from all over the world, and we'll make good money from the venture.''

''But, Zac, could we afford it?''

''I've invested well and made money,'' he assured her. ''I've had no one to spend it on but myself until now. We'll get the property back on its feet and then, if you agree to it, we'll start work on the new venture. We could do a lot of the work ourselves—we're both used to hard work and roughing it.''

''It sounds a wonderful idea.'' The continuing steady rain outside filled her with optimism and the courage to face anything. And with Zac beside her, with old Bazza to help, and Vince and Joanne, two people she would never doubt again, and with extra domestic help when the time came... ''Just as long as my father doesn't interfere.''

His lips brushed hers. ''He won't. My brother was weak, but I'm not. Your father knows it. He's promised not to hassle you anymore—except as an undemanding father and doting grandfather.''

She pursed her lips, her eyes wistful. ''If only!'' It was what she'd always longed for—a loving, undemanding father like other women had—but she still couldn't imagine it ever happening. Did leopards change their spots?

''He means it, dearest. He's decided to sell Barrington's and take life a bit easier—''

"He's decided to *sell?*" She stared at him. "And you believe him?"

"He's going to make an announcement later this week. His doctors have warned him to slow down."

"You mean he really does have a heart problem?"

"He says so, and by his color and overweight, and his age, I'm inclined to believe him." Zac gently kissed the worry from her eyes, first one, then the other, his lips lingering a moment on each fluttering eyelid.

"But without his work he *will* have a heart attack!" she cried. "From sheer boredom." She knew what her workaholic father was like.

"Oh, he'll keep occupied in his retirement. He's talking of setting up a foundation, with a board of directors to help him select causes and charities in need of donations. He knows *we* don't want his money, though he says he'll set up a trust fund for Mikey. Oh, and by the way, my love, he's given us his blessing."

"His blessing!" She looked up at him dazedly. "You've persuaded my father to finally give up and actually give us both his blessing?" It was a miracle. She couldn't believe it. And yet she could—she could believe anything of Zac. He was a man who could make anything happen.

"Word of honor." His eyes danced. "He's going to call you tomorrow and give you his best wishes personally—and his regrets for the pain he's caused you. If you can forgive him, you might like to invite him to our wedding."

Our wedding. Her eyes shone. Her father coming willingly to their wedding would be another miracle.

No. Zac was nothing like Adrian. He never had been. And her father, who'd had Adrian in his pocket, had met his match in Zac. And she'd met her soul mate. Her life partner. The man of her dreams. Wonderful, amazing Zac, her beloved, indomitable gladiator, who'd triumphed over her father and even come away with his blessing.

"Oh, Zac, I hope you can forgive me."

"Forgive you?" Zac smiled, a serene, unworried smile. "Whatever for?"

"For doubting you for so long. For believing what Adrian told me about you. For wondering if…if you wanted Yarrah Downs more than you wanted me. For even wondering if…" She clamped her lips shut, unable to say it. It seemed wicked even to think about it now.

"If…?" He brushed a hand over the silken tangle of her hair. He still didn't look at all worried.

"Oh, Zac, I feel so bad about…about what I did yesterday." She rushed on before she could change her mind. "I was going to clean your travel bag for you and found an old letter inside—the one Adrian sent you at the time he married me. I…I read it."

Zac's dark brows drew down. "I still *have* that letter? Oh, my darling, I would've destroyed it if I'd known it was there. I never meant to keep it. Adrian's gone now, sweetheart. I was hoping you'd never find out, that you'd keep at least some illusions about your husband. He did love you. You were the only woman he ever loved."

"But he loved the idea of my father's money more." She looked up at him with pained eyes. "Oh, Zac, it made me doubt you, too, for a terrible moment! You were Adrian's identical twin—you might have wanted what he wanted. But I didn't believe it, Zac. I *knew* you'd just kept quiet to protect me from the ugly truth about my husband. You didn't want me to know what a grasping gold digger Adrian was."

Her eyes misted with her love for him. "That's the kind of man you are, Zac. You care about people and their feelings. You care about *me*. Bazza speaks so highly of you. And he must know you better than anyone."

"I intend to always be around to care for you, my darling—and Mikey." Zac's lips nuzzled into her hair, his tongue doing erotic things to her left earlobe. "How long do you think it will be before Mikey comes back?" His voice had thickened, and her own was husky as she answered.

"I think that once he's told Buster and Rocky about us, he'll want to tell Bazza and Vince and Jo-anne, and that will take time. Just enough time..." She snuggled closer, curving her body into his and gasping at the instant fire that enveloped her.

"Oh, Zac, I love you!"

"Darling, I love you, too. Heart, body and soul."

She felt a glow inside. All her dreams had come true. She had Mikey safely back home, she had Zac in her life, not just for now but forever, and she still had Yarrah Downs—the only things in life she wanted or would ever want.

Out in the yards and across the paddocks, the rain

was still falling, soaking into the parched earth, re-filling the dams and putting a spring back into the step of the weakened cattle.

Yes, the future, at long last, looked bright.

* * * * *

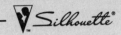

If you enjoyed what you just read,
then we've got an offer you can't resist!

Take 2 bestselling
love stories FREE!
Plus get a FREE surprise gift!

Clip this page and mail it to Silhouette Reader Service™

IN U.S.A.
3010 Walden Ave.
P.O. Box 1867
Buffalo, N.Y. 14240-1867

IN CANADA
P.O. Box 609
Fort Erie, Ontario
L2A 5X3

YES! Please send me 2 free Silhouette Special Edition® novels and my free surprise gift. After receiving them, if I don't wish to receive anymore, I can return the shipping statement marked cancel. If I don't cancel, I will receive 6 brand-new novels every month, before they're available in stores! In the U.S.A., bill me at the bargain price of $3.99 plus 25¢ shipping and handling per book and applicable sales tax, if any*. In Canada, bill me at the bargain price of $4.74 plus 25¢ shipping and handling per book and applicable taxes**. That's the complete price and a savings of at least 10% off the cover prices—what a great deal! I understand that accepting the 2 free books and gift places me under no obligation ever to buy any books. I can always return a shipment and cancel at any time. Even if I never buy another book from Silhouette, the 2 free books and gift are mine to keep forever.

235 SDN DNUR
335 SDN DNUS

Name	(PLEASE PRINT)	
Address	Apt.#	
City	State/Prov.	Zip/Postal Code

* Terms and prices subject to change without notice. Sales tax applicable in N.Y.
** Canadian residents will be charged applicable provincial taxes and GST.
   All orders subject to approval. Offer limited to one per household and not valid to
   current Silhouette Special Edition® subscribers.
® are registered trademarks of Harlequin Books S.A., used under license.

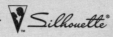

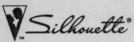

COMING NEXT MONTH

SPECIAL EDITION